ITALIAN AFFAIRS

1977

ENGLISH AS A FUNNY LANGUAGE

DART TRAVIS

Italian Affairs

© Three Vee Limited 2024

threeveeltd.wordpress.com

ISBN for print on demand edition:
978-1-908103-41-3

ISBN for Electronic Version:
978-1-908103-40-6

The characters within this novel are entirely fictional, and if they bear resemblance to any persons, then nothing but coincidence is at play.

Facts purporting to be facts about the external events of 1977 are usually true. If not, they have been thoroughly researched within the imagination of Dart Travis.

Dart Travis's website is at:

http://darttravis.wordpress.com
Cover design by Da Hai
Cover illustration by Ed McLachlan

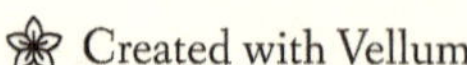 Created with Vellum

CONTENTS

1 / *PRELUDIO*

'Tut'

He shook his head, and tutted again. Malcolm O'Reilly was aware that there were other parking spaces available, but the space with the prominent number 'one' also had a clear sign, 'Director of Studies'. So what was this Ford Escort, in a particularly unpleasant and vibrant shade of blue, doing there? Malcolm O'Reilly slid his beige Saab 99 between a sagging and rusting Hillman Avenger and a shiny new mustard yellow Rover 2000.

O'Reilly climbed out of the driver's seat, and straightened his jacket and trousers. Crumpled was not his favoured sartorial choice. He glanced in the window of the offensively parked Ford. Cardboard boxes filled the back seat adorned with the letters UUP and the coat of arms of United Universities Press. That placed the owner.

He had seen the Rover 2000 before. Bernard Arnold's car. Arnold was Director of Studies at Euro-Lang, the largest rival English Language School, though it was not as large nor as prestigious as WEC, O'Reilly's World English Centre.

'Tut.' The Rover was undoubtedly a company car. O'Reilly made a mental note to approach his Swiss directors on the subject of upgrading his own vehicle. A Rover 2000 was a provincial bank manager choice. He had read an article with cartoons linking cars to people. Saab was 'architects, authors and doctors,' all categories which O'Reilly considered to be his peers. A new larger Saab was due next year, the 900. Perhaps a Turbo version of that model for his next Saab would suffice. It would not do to be outclassed by Euro-Lang. He chuckled to himself. He always thought of Bernard as Benedict Arnold. Perhaps he could make the same error this evening in conversation.

The event was taking place in the school restaurant. O'Reilly had been most reluctant to allow it on the premises of WEC, but the sales representative had kept badgering him with phone calls until he agreed to the book launch. After all, the author was one of his own staff, and the ancient imprint of United Universities Press brought an academic sheen to its publications, whether deserved or not. In this case, thought O'Reilly, 'definitely not.' O'Reilly had carefully delayed his own arrival so as to avoid chit chat, and also to make something of an entrance. Mrs Tupper was perfectly capable of welcoming the teachers from the other ... lesser, O'Reilly added mentally ... local language schools. He doubted that many of his own staff would feel tempted to spend an evening listening to their most boring and universally disliked colleague, although the provision of free wine and a finger buffet by the publisher might prove a sufficient attraction.

The buffet was laid out on trestle tables with paper tablecloths along the side of the room. There were at least fifty teachers assembled there. A great surprise, though as expected, few of them were his own employees. He noted Pamela with a glass of orange squash. She'd be there out of misguided loyalty, and the fact that she'd have nothing else to do.

'Mr O'Reilly! A pleasure. A great pleasure, to be sure.'

O'Reilly recognised the accent at once, 'Mr O'Toole,' he said politely. He wondered why the representative of such an august publishing house saw fit to wear creased corduroy trousers and a chunky sweater on the occasion.

'A fellow Irishman, *Dia duit.*'

'Not exactly,' said Malcolm O'Reilly, 'It is rather a lengthy tale. Eastern European ancestors. Their name was Oraizski and they simplified it.'

'Good on them, so. I don't have the Gaelic meself,' said O'Toole, 'Just trying to impress you with my erudition. But fuck that for a game of soldiers. Call me Patrick ...'

'Malcolm ...' O'Reilly replied stiffly. He filled the silence, 'This is our first book launch.'

'Mine too. I only joined the press a couple of months ago. They need a fecking good kick up the arse, to be honest.'

'Such is the case with so many venerable institutions,' said O'Reilly, 'The Civil Service, the National Theatre ...'

'I'm responsible for UK language schools,' Patrick continued, 'Not for long. I got this job to get about overseas. I'm thinking France. They love the Irish. Still, for now, I'm stuck with promoting yer man Graham Donaldson in England. Can you believe they let the fecker call the book *Intercourse*?'

'I had commented on the title all too often myself. He insists it means Intermediate Course coupled with the sense of a conversation.'

'So it's not about the riding, then? I'll have to change the thrust of my promotion.'

The gesture on 'thrust' was unnecessary. O'Reilly laughed politely, 'Indeed not. I recall that H.G. Wells in *First Men In The Moon* had characters saying, "I must have intercourse with the Selenites." We had to read it aloud, with being sent to the headmaster for the cane for laughing. Are you familiar with it?'

'I am, so. I was an English teacher back in Dublin,' said Patrick,

'I'm afraid I may have parked in your space, Malcolm. I hope it's not inconvenient. It was a closer walk with the boxes of books.'

'Not at all,' said O'Reilly. About twenty yards closer at most, he thought.

'Well, go on, Malcolm, get yourself outside a glass of wine now,' Patrick indicated the buffet.

'How kind,' murmured O'Reilly. Fortunately the World English Centre catering staff had been commissioned to prepare the buffet. He would have to check that Mrs Tupper had invoiced UUP.

Bernard Arnold was talking to Pamela. For a moment, O'Reilly felt irritated. Was Arnold trying to poach his staff? Then he reflected that he might not be too displeased to lose Pamela's services. While he treasured her sycophancy, he dreaded getting caught in conversation with her at coffee breaks. Her fondness for describing how very sweet her Arab students were, was combined with detailed and repetitive descriptions of their predictable language errors which she found endearing. Arnold was dressed in a dull brown tweed jacket as usual. Why did these people feel they had to dress up as teachers? O'Reilly was immaculate in his dove grey suit with a pale pink shirt and a subtle cream silk tie.

'Pamela,' said O'Reilly, 'Thank you so much for coming.' He wondered whether that was lettuce adhering to her front tooth, or whether it had simply starting rotting.

'I wouldn't miss it for the world, Malcolm!' she enthused, 'Think! Graham being published by UUP! And I've known him all these years.'

O'Reilly pondered. Graham Donaldson had kept himself squirrelled away in a corner, avoided the staff restaurant at break times, prided himself on being anti-social, and point-blank refused to show anyone the material he was writing and teaching.

'Benedict,' said O'Reilly, and nodded, 'Oh, I'm so awfully sorry.

It's virtually Tourette's syndrome with your surname. Bernard, of course.'

Bernard Arnold glared, 'Evening, Malcolm,' he held up his glass, 'Did WEC supply the wine?'

'Alas no,' said O'Reilly, 'We offered, but UUP supplied the beverages.'

'Tesco Spanish Red,' said Arnold, and sniffed, 'Truman Education had Beaujolais-Villages and Macon blanc at their book launch for *Passports* at Euro-Lang.'

O'Reilly surveyed the bunch of teachers eagerly waiting for refills, jostling to get to the bottles. The expression 'Pearls before swine,' came to mind.

Bernard Arnold took a bite of the quarter sandwich, 'The nibbles aren't bad. Processed cheese though.'

Nibbles! It was a term that O'Reilly had always considered particularly vulgar. 'Emmental. Perhaps you're unfamiliar with the Swiss Alpine cheeses,' he responded.

'By the way, Malcolm, what was that advert about for summer course teachers in the Evening Echo?'

'We run extensive summer courses. You know that.'

'That's not what I meant,' said Bernard Arnold, 'It's the line "We pay more than any other local language school."'

'We do.'

'Bob Spooner from The Queen's English Academy was on the phone about it. You have exactly the same sentence advertising for host families. No one benefits from that sort of bidding war for staff or accommodation.'

'Again, Bernard, we certainly do. You could always try and match us.'

'Euro-Lang's a charitable organisation. We're not in this for profit.'

'Bollocks, Bernard,' said O'Reilly cheerfully, 'Of course you are. If you'll excuse me, I must check a few details with Mrs Tupper.'

O'Reilly was pleased with his own restraint. It had been

tempting to mention the number of Euro-Lang teachers who had applied to him for jobs in the last few weeks. There were several he would love to employ in preference to his existing staff. However he had no vacancies at present.

O'Reilly was gratified to see that Mrs Tupper was wearing an elegant eau-de-nil skirt suit with a cream silk blouse and a discrete string of pearls, though the gold spectacles on a gold chain and pale mauve hair tint detracted somewhat. Still, she was a credit to the school.

'You look very smart, Mrs Tupper,' he said.

'As do you, Mr O'Reilly,' she replied, 'As ever. Have you spoken to that oik from the publisher yet?'

'I have.'

'He's most uncouth. He used, well, an obscenity in my presence.'

O'Reilly tutted. It was an evening for tutting, 'Oh, dear. I must apologize for exposing you to that.'

'I do hope the directors never discover that we were serving cheap supermarket wine in litre bottles,' she said.

'However, not to our staff,' said O'Reilly, 'I've only seen Pamela so far, and she eschews alcohol.'

'I do wish they'd let us cater for the drinks as well. We have some gorgeous Swiss Petite Arvine white wine in the store.'

O'Reilly watched a nearby teacher sink a brimming large glass of Tesco Hungarian White in one gulp, 'I'm sure UUP know their market. Is Donaldson here yet?'

'He's waiting in the Intermediate staff room. Mr O'Toole thought he should make an entrance for his presentation.'

'Waiting or skulking?'

Mrs Tupper tittered.

Patrick O'Toole walked to the front and clapped his hands, 'Ladies and gentlemen! And others. Now's the time to refill your glasses …

get a good top up before we start. Go on. We're not counting how many glasses you get down you. For those who can write, there'll be no need to take notes because United Universities Press has madly agreed to present everyone here tonight with a complimentary copy of Graham Donaldson's new publication, so. Graham will be talking on Prescriptive Grammar versus Descriptive Grammar. For those who don't have a fecking clue, prescriptive grammar is all that anally-retentive shite elderly schoolmasters in black gowns drummed into you with a cane, like not ending your sentences with a preposition. A rule up with which I will not put, as Winston Churchill once said. Descriptive grammar is how youse feckers actually use it in real life, though fair's fair, I personally may not be your best example. But enough shite about me. So, may I present our esteemed author, Graham Donaldson!'

O'Reilly was aware that Patrick had avoided saying the title aloud, also that he'd grabbed everyone's attention with his exaggerated stage Irishman act. He also had to admit that in the few times Donaldson ever bothered to venture an opinion, it had been on accepting language change, and O'Reilly had had to agree with him. It had generated clashes with old Lieutenant-Colonel Trevelyan, a staff member who O'Reilly would dearly love to get rid of.

Graham Donaldson shuffled into the restaurant. Scuffed suede shoes, crumpled grey terylene trousers, and crumpled and shabby tweed jacket with elbow patches. Grey shirt with a blue college tie ... teacher training college, in O'Reilly's memory.

Graham tapped the microphone, coughed wetly, and started assembling his notes on the lectern. A minute passed.

'Good evening. I shall be ... er ... demonstrating ... some, um, exercises, and er, indeed, grammatical, um, structural explanations of, um, points of grammatical structure...'

O'Reilly smiled. Yes, Graham Donaldson was just as inept a public speaker as he had imagined he would be.

Graham drew a deep breath, 'So I'll begin by demonstrating *Intercourse* to you ...'

It was two weeks later.

The intercom on his desk buzzed. O'Reilly pressed the button, 'Yes, Mrs Tupper?'

'Mr Donaldson is here to see you, Mr O'Reilly.'

'Please send him in.'

Graham Donaldson came in. He perused the theatre programmes from Llandudno, Morecambe and Stoke-on-Trent on the walls, venues where O'Reilly had once performed in, or at least produced plays, and then the meticulously tidy desk with its neat row of pens. 'Thank you for seeing me, um, Malcolm.'

'How can I be of help, Graham?'

'I received a telephone call from my editor at UUP ... Giles Winthrop. It seems they have a request for me to attend a conference in Italy. It's on a Saturday and Sunday.'

O'Reilly pursed his lips, 'Given WEC's generous holiday provision, there should be no problem in taking the Friday and Monday off as part of your entitlement.'

Graham coughed, 'It's a new major conference. Two thousand teachers expected. It's in Rome. Apparently, Italy is starting a mass in-service teacher training programme in English Language. They ... UUP, that is ... wish me to participate. The thing is, they want me to do a week's tour before the conference. All round Italy.'

'So you wish to arrange a week of your annual leave?'

'Not exactly. They ... UUP ... think that it would benefit WEC to be associated with *Intercourse* and, well, allow me the time.'

O'Reilly frowned, 'I suppose this is O'Toole's idea.'

'Not at all. Nothing to do with him. The request comes from their Italian office in Milan. Incidentally, I cannot believe that a school, even one situated in Dublin, would have employed such a fellow.'

'I disagree,' said O'Reilly, 'Though acerbic and in many ways abrasive, and fraudulent, Patrick O'Toole is both stimulating and persuasive. He has a certain charisma. I'd employ him.'

'Good Lord,' responded Graham, 'Really?'

'Absolutely. As you may have noticed, enthusiasm and communication ability are as important as linguistic knowledge. That is why our ex-teachers like dear Roger Fleetwood with an acting background were so treasured.' Like myself, O'Reilly added mentally. He wondered how Roger was getting on in California. San Francisco should suit him.

Graham said, 'Teachers in Italy are converting from French teaching to English teaching and there's such an enormous demand for training, according to UUP.'

'Teacher training?' O'Reilly snorted, 'You have always declined to share your knowledge of grammar on the teacher training courses here.'

Teacher training had become important both for WEC's own staff, and for the January 'Southern Hemisphere summer' courses that they ran for teachers from Brazil, Argentina, Uruguay and Chile. O'Reilly reflected, the take up for the July and August courses for European teachers had been most disappointing. 'I have a proposal. If we allow you the time, UUP must undertake to give fliers advertising our courses to all participants. They must also introduce you as from World English Centre, Bournemouth.' O'Reilly was not relying on Graham's performance so much as the tacit seal of UUP's ancient reputation upon the training courses.

'I should have to ask Giles ...'

'Or you could take the time as part of your annual leave instead.'

'I'll tell Giles.'

'I thought you might. Are the teachers across the whole spectrum, or does the training lean more to *scuola media* or *scuola media superiore*?

'What?'

O'Reilly sighed, 'Lower secondary or upper secondary?'

'I have absolutely no idea. I've never been to Italy.'

'Then you might ask Barry.'

'Who?'

'Your colleague. Barry Grant. For goodness sake, Graham, you have been sharing a staff room with him for the last five years.'

'Ah, Grant. Of course.'

'His fiancée, Gabriella, is approaching the end of her English and Linguistics degree in Bologna. You must remember her. Sweet girl. Very bright too. You were her class teacher for three months when she was here.'

'The faces and names blur. Was she Italian?'

'Gabriella ... Bologna ... the clues indicate that she is. Well, do have a chat with Barry. I'm sure he'll brief you on the Italian education system.'

Graham closed the door behind him.

O'Reilly picked up the phone, 'Mrs Tupper? Could you put me through to Dr Schaffhauser at head office in Switzerland? I have an idea.'

Hans-Jurgen Schaffhauser was most impressed at Malcolm O'Reilly's suggestion. It was going far better than O'Reilly had anticipated.

'After all these years, er, Malcolm, I must now invite you to call me Hans-Jurgen.'

'I'm honoured, Hans-Jurgen. There are two thousand English teachers expected in Rome, as I mentioned. I assume we will need to reserve a table at the book exhibition where we can advertise our teacher training courses, and I can be there in person to explain and hopefully sign people up. It's by no means unprecedented. The

British Council, International House and Bell Cambridge do much the same. Not that they have a Director of Studies to do it.'

'Mr Donaldson will be speaking at the conference? I remember him as a quiet chap,' Schaffhauser's voice radiated pride in his choice of the word 'chap', 'One who would not say boo to a duck.'

'Goose,' said O'Reilly, 'The exact expression is boo to a goose, though you expressed the thought perfectly. I had considered that, but he is sound on modern interpretations of grammar, and I suspect that will go down well in Italy.'

'I agree. As with Swiss-Germans, the Italians like grammar rules. Even more,' said Schaffhauser, 'You should try to persuade teachers to bring parties of students to WEC also. You can offer the usual commission plus a free place on the teacher training course if they will bring ten ... no, fifteen students ... and increase the commission by five per cent if it is needed to cement the arrangement.'

'What a superb idea,' said O'Reilly, who had been about to suggest it himself.

'Yes. You must go, Malcolm,' Schaffhauser said, 'And as you will be giving up your weekend free time to work for us, I will ask if you would like to take Mrs O'Reilly with you. The hotel price will be little difference for two persons or one, and I'm sure we should ... would?'

'Either,' said O'Reilly.

'Thank you. We would be happy to pay her air fare as well as to pay your air fare.'

'That is most kind, Dr Schaffhauser. Gloria will be thrilled.'

'Hans-Jurgen, remember. Also a per diem for meals. And a minimum of four star accommodation.'

'How very generous.'

2 / VOLARE

Graham Donaldson had flown before, but not for some years. He
closed his eyes as the plane bumped through cloud and swooped in
towards the airport. The pain in his ears was sharp and sudden and
persistent. The plump fellow in the middle seat was saying
something to him. It was a distant blur, 'What?'

'leedle dowa reeser …' the fellow was pointing out of the window.

Graham glanced sideways … trees and buildings were racing past
the window at a sickening pace. There was a sudden painful pop and
his ears filled with the roar of the engines, 'What?'

'Leaning Tower of Pisa,' said the fat fellow.

'You missed it,' said his even plumper wife, who was in the
window seat, 'You can see it on the way in. It's still leaning alright.'

There was a terrific bump as the wheels slammed onto the
runway. 'Ooh!' Graham squeaked.

The tannoy boomed out, *'Please remain in your seats until the
aircraft has come to a complete standstill and the captain has switched
off the fasten seat belt signs.'*

'Scuse me, chum.'

'Eh?'

The man had unclipped his seat belt and was starting to struggle to his feet.

'Er, you're supposed to wait until ...'

'Want to get my bags. Get out first,' said the man, 'The Ities are so slow at passport control, it's best to be at the front of the queue. Idle bastards,' he added.

'Could you please sit down?' it was the air hostess, 'It's a regulation.'

'You're standing, luv.'

'That's my job.'

The man slumped back into his seat, 'That's the trouble with British Airways,' he said, 'Officious bitches, the lot of them.'

'Mmm,' said Graham as quietly as he could.

'Should of come Alitalia. They don't give a bugger about you standing up. Everyone does it.'

'Should have,' murmured Graham to himself. He'd thought this before. It was increasingly prevalent among the British, though it was not an error foreign students ever made. Perhaps 'should of' and 'would of' needed to be noted for recognition in grammar summaries, marked maybe as 'common native speaker error'? One made by the more common sort of native speaker. He would have to give it some thought.

'We got a villa. In Tuscany. Come several times a year.'

'Very pleasant,' said Graham. He wondered why total strangers should see fit to describe their vacation habits to him, particularly in such a strong Midlands accent.

'It's a bit miserable this time of the season. Bloody foggy up there in the hills, but you can't rent it out in November, and so we come over and do a spot of maintenance. Can't trust Itie plumbers. I'm a plumber myself. I got high standards.'

'I'm sure you have,' ventured Graham.

'We've had a lot of trouble with the bogs. You should see what people stuff down them.'

'Terrible,' said his wife, 'And we've got packs of sanitary bags in the bathroom and the downstairs one.'

The seat belt lights went off. Everyone stood.

'Watch your head,' said the man as he reached across Graham to the overhead locker, 'My bag weighs a ton. See, they don't weigh hand baggage ... they just check the size.'

'Yeah,' said the wife, pushing past Graham, 'Two bags full; HP Sauce, Marmite, Colman's Mustard, Dairy Milk chocolate, Typhoo tea, McVities Digestives. You can't get any of it in Florence. Our clientele appreciate some home comforts in the Welcome Packs.'

'You can get ketchup easy enough there,' said her husband, 'Though when all's said and done, it's fine on hot dogs with some onions, but you wouldn't put ketchup on a good fry up, would you? I wouldn't, chum. You need brown sauce.'

Graham nodded nervously, 'I suppose so ...'

The man struggled with the bag, which clattered alarmingly, then pulled a card from his jacket pocket, 'There you are, chum,' he said, 'That's our phone number in Wolverhampton. Next Italian holiday, come and give the villa a try. Very romantic setting ... bring a lady friend. Two bedrooms, plus a couple of Put-U-Ups downstairs. You can get a pasta dinner in the village, if you like that sort of thing, but we've got a fully equipped kitchen for when you want some decent English grub.'

'Thank you,' said Graham, 'Um, I'm supposed to get some sort of shuttle bus from Pisa Airport into Florence. Do you know anything about where it goes from?'

'Course we do. We're on it ourselves, chum. You stick with us ... I'm Mike, and this is Phyllis. We'll see you alright.'

Graham had heard as much about plumbing and drains as he had ever wanted to know on the hour's bus ride. Mike had elected to sit next to him while Phyllis read a magazine in the seat behind. He explained that he had four vans in his drainage company, and couldn't get apprentices nowadays for any amount of money, and that plastic gloves were no incentive for younger workers to shove their hands down a blocked toilet.

'Different generation, Graham,' he said (they had established his name and were on first name terms), 'When you was in the war, you got used to a bit of shit and worse. That's how come we bought the villa. I was here in 1944, loved the place. Looked like flaming paradise after the North African campaign. We thought about buying one on the beach in Spain, but it's not the same. I saw enough sand in Egypt to last me a lifetime. Phyllis got very upset about the way they treat donkeys and the bullfighting in Spain too. She's right soft on animals. Mind you, most of the English out here in Tuscany are snotty buggers. Drive their Jags and Mercs ... and Ferraris and Astons some of them ... all the way from England. We've got a Fiat 127 in the garage at the villa. Keep it there on a trickle charger. We'll get a taxi up there from Florence. Ordinary car. We like to blend in with the locals, see. Well, unless I've got my England football shirt on.'

Graham watched them waddle off to the taxi rank with their luggage and peered around. He had been told he would be met at the bus terminal. It was bad enough being made to find his own way from Pisa Airport to Florence, let alone to be abandoned on a Sunday afternoon, in a bus station full of foreigners, suitcase in one hand, briefcase in the other. He realised that UUP hadn't even told him where he would be staying. What was he supposed to do if no one turned up?

A woman was pushing her way through the queue at the taxi rank. Black curly hair. Tartan skirt and jacket ... and thank goodness, she was holding a copy of *Intercourse* aloft.

'Dr Donaldson!' she shouted.

A wave of relief swept over him. She hurried over.

'Welcome to Florence! My name is Francesca Garibaldi from United Universities Press. I'm so happy to greet you.'

Graham sniffed, 'I was more than somewhat perturbed to find no one here.'

Francesca noticed the lack of a return greeting, 'My apologies. My taxi was stuck in the traffic.' He was still scowling. She felt obliged to continue, 'I was lunching with my mother. She is quite elderly and naturally everything was delayed. Sunday lunch is my tradition with her. I am so sorry. How should I address you, as Dr Donaldson, or would you prefer Graham?'

Graham wondered whether to correct the misapplied doctorate. Perhaps it was easier not to. 'Um, Graham is fine.'

'Then you should call me Francesca.'

'Did you say your surname was Garibaldi? Like the biscuit?'

'Like Giuseppe Garibaldi, the great Italian patriot,' Francesca said firmly, 'It is quite a common name in Genova and the Liguria region,' she paused, 'So, do you speak Italian?'

'No.'

'Then it will be an opportunity to exercise my English. Incidentally, I am always keen to improve. You must correct me if I should make mistakes.'

'Your English is very good,' said Graham. Did the woman expect him to give her English lessons?

'I hope so,' she said, 'I used to teach English in Switzerland, and in France.'

'So you were a language teacher?'

'Yes,' what a rude man he was. Her eyes glinted, 'I have also taught Italian in Germany, and French in England … in Basingstoke. Do you know it?'

'Not really.'

'Jane Austen was born there,' Francesca said.

'I see,' said Graham. He wondered why foreigners were so eager to demonstrate knowledge of English literary figures.

'And I taught German here in Italy,' she finished, 'Languages are like a hobby to me. So we share a common interest, I hope. Come, we will take a taxi to your hotel.'

She strode forward. Graham struggled behind with suitcase and briefcase. If they'd sent a man to meet him, he could at least have insisted he carry them.

They joined the line for taxis.

'We have booked a very special hotel. James was delighted with it.'

'Who on Earth is James?' snapped Graham.

'The managing director of UUP.'

'Ah. Yes, yes. I have met him.' Extremely tall, Graham recalled. White hair. Advanced RP public school accent.

'It's a fourteenth century building, an old palace in a narrow Florentine street. The Monna Lisa. It's very beautiful. I'm not staying there myself. I always stay with my mother in Florence, which is why it is convenient to begin tours here.'

'You mean convenient for you?' said Graham testily, 'It's not convenient from the airport at Pisa.'

'Convenient for UUP. They do not have to pay for my accommodation,' explained Francesca, 'Nor my travel here from Milan.' She had been looking forward to this week's tour, but the signs so far were not promising. Perhaps when he'd had time to relax and wash he might be more amenable.

The taxi stopped outside a massive wooden door in a narrow street. It must have been twelve feet high. A small brass sign announced the name.

'Good ... do you have your passport? I must register you. Then I shall give you time to freshen up. Would seven-thirty be a good time to collect you for dinner? Yes?'

'I suppose so,' said Graham. So he was to be abandoned for two hours with nothing to do.

· · ·

The room was dark, the heavy oak shutters firmly closed over the windows. One light bulb overhead. Twenty watts at the most. The porter had hovered for a good two minutes wittering about times for breakfast before Graham finally said 'Excuse me' and closed the door on him. After a tip, of course. Grasping fellow. The panting and heavy breathing carrying his case and briefcase up the stairway had been theatrical. The floor was bare tiles apart from a small rug next to the bed. It would be cold underfoot. A huge and ancient wardrobe with its ornate painted patterns towered over the bed which looked too soft and lumpy to Graham. Fourteenth century straw perhaps. He snickered at his own humour. Dark oil paintings of buildings in gold frames on the walls. An ugly and hirsute fellow in a gold metal helmet was framed opposite the bed. He hauled his suitcase onto the bed and opened it. Filthy, those Italian stations and streets, he thought. You could see the black marks his case had left all over the bed cover. He pushed open the dark door to the windowless bathroom. The sink was heavy and ornate. No sign of a chain on the water closet. So how did one flush it? He tried the button set in the tiled wall. That did the trick. A curved bath with a shower over it. Rust marks led down from the ridiculously baroque taps. Most unsatisfactory. Much too dark. He thought of opening the shutters, but the catches looked complex. He had disliked the way the receptionist had kept hold of his passport too. 'It will be returned in the morning,' he was told. Dinner at 7.30? He could imagine the pizza with cheap red wine. He'd had enough of that back in Bournemouth during those interminable and compulsory class farewell parties at WEC.

Graham sat down grumpily in a huge leather chair in reception at seven twenty-five. He fully expected the Garibaldi woman to arrive late. Garibaldi takes the biscuit! He thought and chuckled to himself.

He wondered whether to cross the lobby and examine the rack of brochures on the other side, but after all, he was not a tourist.

Francesca arrived on the dot of seven-thirty. Graham noted that she'd changed into some sort of bright turquoise floral frock, and a small jacket. Huge earrings. Typical woman. She would be trying to show him up.

Francesca wondered why Graham had not at least shaved and changed his shirt and shabby tie for dinner. The man had had two hours to have a shower. She felt mildly insulted.

'It's a short walk,' said Francesca, 'It's a pleasant restaurant. The local office almost uses it as their office canteen.' She saw his expression. Maybe 'canteen' was not a good word to have chosen.

'Do UUP have an office in Florence?' he said in surprise.

'Our distributor and collaborator. NIE ... Nord Italia Editrice. They have offices in every major town. You'll be seeing a lot of them, starting tomorrow. My role is partly co-ordinating between UUP and NIE though we have our own UUP office in Milan. NIE are most enthusiastic about your new book.'

The restaurant's walls were completely covered by paintings. There were three rows of them on each wall, different styles, shapes and sizes, hung just an inch or two a part in a wide variety of frames. They were shown to a table by the window.

'This will be most fascinating,' she said, 'There is a restaurant competition this week in Florence and today is the first day. All the dishes must be pre-Columbian. Like your hotel room, you will experience fourteenth century Florence.'

'Pre-Columbian? I don't understand.'

'It means they may not use any ingredients that were brought to Italy after the discovery of the Americas,' Francesca paused, 'So no tomatoes, no potatoes, no peppers, no chilis, no runner beans, no ...' she searched her mind, 'No avocados. No chocolate. No turkey.

However, I don't think Marco Polo's earlier imports are banned. Therefore we may still get spaghetti,' she laughed.

'No tomatoes?' said Graham, 'So there's no pizza on tonight's menu.'

'This class of restaurant does not serve pizza, obviously,' said Francesca in surprise.

'I thought all Italian restaurants did.'

'No,' said Francesca, 'Though I will take you for pizza in Napoli ... Naples.'

A man in a white apron hurried across the restaurant, arms outstretched. Francesca stood, and they embraced and kissed on both cheeks.

'*Ciao Bella!*' said the man and indicated her dress and went into fast Italian.

Francesca blushed, then she was smiling, '*Grazie a lei,*' she said, and there was another flurry of Italian.

Graham thought it most inconsiderate. Not only did the woman arrange the tour to suit her family obligations, but it was clear that UUP's expense budget was going to a friend of hers. The man was nodding. He turned to Graham, 'Welcome to Firenze!'

'This is Giovanni,' said Francesca, 'He is the owner and the chef. He doesn't speak English. He apologises to you for this.'

'Welcome to Firenze!' said Giovanni again.

'This is all the English he speaks,' she said. She returned to Italian. Giovanni answered at length, while Francesca nodded. She turned to Graham, 'There is no printed menu tonight.'

Giovanni spoke again.

Francesca laughed, 'For there were no printing presses in the fourteenth century, he says. And few could read.'

Giovanni produced another stream of voluble Italian.

Francesca smiled, 'However as we are his special friends, he will permit the use of a knife and fork. Really you should bring your own knife ... or dagger ... and use it. I will translate the menu ... first there is a choice of soup or *cinghiale*,' she paused to find the words, 'Yes, wild boar ham ...'

'Soup,' said Graham.

'Are you absolutely sure? It's ...'

'I should like soup,' repeated Graham firmly. You shouldn't have to say these things twice.

She shrugged, 'Then it will be venison cooked with forest berries and pears, served with old-fashioned rye and barley bread. It sounds very good indeed.'

'Yes, yes,' said Graham, 'That's fine.'

'The dessert will be pears also, with hazelnuts and honey ... we are usually seasonal in Italy anyway, but in those days they could only be seasonal. No choices. The wine he serves will be local Tuscan novella ... the first wine of 1977. You must know Beaujolais Nouveau? It is similar. He says they rarely aged wine in the fourteenth century. He says it will taste young and a little sharp but is authentic.'

Francesca explained the week's tour route carefully. Giovanni arrived with a thick wooden platter, a huge knife and a large chunk of meat with skin and black tufts of hair on one side and a huge bone in the middle.

'The wild boar ham,' she said, 'I ordered it.'

Giovanni placed a bowl in front of Graham, and spoke in Italian.

'This is a fourteenth century speciality,' she translated, 'It is olive oil soup with garlic and bread ... croutons, I suppose.'

'Like French Onion soup?' he said.

'Not quite. I think it is just hot olive oil in fact, but it will be a fine quality one. Be careful, the bowl is very hot.'

She watched him guzzling it, 'Perhaps you would like to use the napkin?' she suggested, 'Olive oil is most difficult to remove from the fabric of your clothing.'

. . .

Halfway through the main course, Graham was convinced that it was the best meal he had ever had in his life. The conversation had turned to his companions on the bus, and he had mentioned 'would of' and 'should of.'

'Indeed. I had noticed this in Basingstoke,' said Francesca, 'My pupils often said it. You will not see this error in Italian pupils. This is because the English children have never been taught the grammar of their own language. Why, even past tense and present tense was a new concept for them. The English teachers worry about clause analysis, and we French teachers ... or rather in my case, teachers of French ... had to explain English tense grammar to English pupils.'

The meal went well. Graham was surprised when the chef ... Giovanni ... sat and joined them at their table after the bill had been paid. He had brought a bottle of grappa and three glasses. Still, he seemed a convivial fellow, the grappa was warming, and his cooking had been superb.

Graham Donaldson squirmed in the chair in the lobby of the *Monna Lisa*. His suitcase was beside him. They were to carry it around the entire day before catching an evening train to Milan. Dreadful planning. An American couple were at the reception desk.

'I hope you have enjoyed your stay with us,' the receptionist had said.

The American man's voice boomed out, 'Sure. The first two nights were great. Last night was not so good. We couldn't sleep. Someone in the room above us was marching about and flushing the water closet every twenty minutes. Not your fault,' he added, 'We thought it was seriously lacking in consideration for other hotel guests.'

Graham squirmed again. He had already handed his room key in. He really would need to use the facilities in the lobby, not that there was any toilet paper left in his room. Both rolls and the two packets of Kleenex tissues in his briefcase had been used up. He had been beset with dreams between visits to the bathroom which harked back to Mike's vivid descriptions of drainage problems. The coffee and croissant had resurrected the griping feeling. In retrospect, consuming a third of a pint of hot olive oil with garlic had been an error, and the young wine had not helped.

He stood up and looked into the bar area. Good, two doors. One was inscribed *Signore* in gold letters and the other *Signori*. What an absurd language! The bar was dark at this time of day and many people would never notice the subtle difference. There were no symbols. Well, as a language specialist, Graham remembered being addressed as *Signore*. He pushed open the door. The woman at the basin gave a small scream. He backed out. So was *signori* the gents? He was relieved to see there were urinals as well as cubicles. And then relieved. Hopefully there could be no more.

Graham regained his seat and looked at his watch. Nine-thirty, she had said last night. It was already nine thirty-six. Annoying. Typical woman. Typical Italian, he expected.

That was when Francesca emerged from the back office, 'Good morning, Graham,' she said brightly, 'I trust you slept well.'

'Mmm. Morning,' he said.

'I was here at nine-twenty. I saw your suitcase in the lobby, but I couldn't find you. I've had a most useful time. I paid your account, and have arranged for a future UUP discount as we use this hotel quite often. Now, Mario from NIE will be taking us today. We'll keep your suitcase secure in his car. I've arranged something special for this morning. One of the local *superiore*, or upper secondary schools, has agreed that you can observe a lesson! What do you think? It will give such a good opportunity to become acquainted with the schools here. Let's go... or as we say in Italian, *Andiamo!*'

They stood in the imposing hotel doorway and Francesca waved to a car at the junction two hundred metres away, which was parked entirely across a pedestrian crossing. The car moved forward, and the driver got out. Smart beige suit.

'*Buongiorno*, Dottore Donaldson. I am Mario Vitale from Nord Italia Editrice. Welcome to Firenze ... please you must to excuse my too bad English. Allow me to take your case ... you must to sit in the front. There is more space for the legs.'

Two vans and a car were now stuck behind Mario's car in the ancient narrow street, and three car horns were blaring out.

Mario was slowly and carefully adjusting the boxes of books in the boot to squeeze Graham's suitcase in. Francesca waited patiently for him to finish and to open the back door for her, before gracefully getting in. Graham wondered why the woman was incapable of opening the door herself. Mario opened the front passenger door for him with a flourish. There were now half a dozen vehicles behind them with horns blaring.

'*Prego, Dottore ...*'

Mario got in and pulled away. He turned right into an even narrower street. Graham looked in alarm at the road signs, 'This is a one way street! We're going along it the wrong way!' he said.

'No problem,' said Mario, 'Is only short one.'

A van had turned into the street from the opposite direction. Mario tapped his horn and waved, and the van reversed back around the corner to allow him through.

Francesca sensed Graham's trepidation and leaned forward, 'It's common in Florence. The streets are so narrow, and you must go a long way around. If everyone obeyed the regulations, traffic would not get anywhere,' she said.

'This is true,' said Mario, 'Are you comfortable, *Dottore*? Would you like some music? I have the cassette of *Rumors*?'

'Rumours? I don't understand. What kind of rumours?'

'Fleetwood Mac,' explained Francesca.

'Uh, no thank you,' said Graham, 'I'd rather sit quietly.'

The marble floors of the wide dark corridor were cold. Mario led them past some sort of canteen. It seemed full of teenagers who were smoking and chatting. No school uniform here, Graham observed.

He was dreading this. Why on Earth did they imagine he wanted to see a class full of unpleasant foreign teenagers?

The teacher, Signora Ferrara was waiting for them. She was a stout woman with steely grey stiffly permed hair and a she had a carefully arranged scarf around her neck, pinned with a gold brooch.

'*Buongiorno*, Dottore Donaldson,' she said.

Graham tried to remember an Italian greeting ... there had been enough Italians at WEC after all. '*Ciao*,' he said, then remembered the greeting to Francesca in the restaurant last night, '*Ciao Bella.*'

Francesca winced. Mario was trying desperately to stifle a laugh.

Signora Ferrara shook her head, 'If you would like to follow me.'

Mario immediately engaged her in conversation.

Francesca hung back, and tapped Graham's arm, 'Graham. You do not speak any Italian, so please do not try. Not ever. Stick with English. You have just addressed the Head of the English Department, a dignified lady in her late fifties, and a good translation of what you just said might be "Hi, gorgeous."'

Signora Ferrara stopped outside the classroom, from which considerable noise was emanating, 'This is their first year in *superiore*. They have all studied English in *scuola media*, but for not enough time, and with insufficient rigour. They now have four hours a week,' she paused, 'I have been examining your *Intercourse* text. It is good for the better classes in *superiore*, I believe.'

'In fact, for adults and young adults in private lang ...'started Graham.

'Exactly, Signora Ferrara,' said Francesca, stepping in front of him, 'It has been designed and written with this level of *superiore* at the forefront.'

'Thank you for confirming, Signorina Garibaldi. This was my mind also.'

Graham opened and closed his mouth.

'So we will leave you with Signora Ferrara,' said Francesca to Graham, 'Signor Vitale and I have an appointment with the headmaster.'

Graham watched them depart along the corridor, Francesca's heels clacking on the marble.

Signora Ferrara smiled at him grimly, 'Signor Vitale has explained your error, and that you do not speak Italian, and that United Universities Press have specialists advisors for each language.'

'Er, that's ... um, correct,' lied Graham.

'You will see I conduct my class entirely in English. The Direct Method, which I think is your method with *Intercourse*. You do it directly. Even to the point, that the pupils will address me as "Miss" even though I am in fact a Mrs. I have noted that English pupils must address all lady teachers as Miss, with no regard to their marital status.'

'Quite true,' mumbled Graham. That had never struck him before. Perhaps a note in the Teacher's Book was called for.

Signora Ferrara opened the door. There was instant silence. She smiled, 'Let us enter.'

Everyone stood up.

'Good morning, Miss,' chorused the class.

'Good morning,' she replied, 'I have the honour to introduce Doctor Donaldson, a very famous English author and university professor.' She indicated him.

'Good morning, Doctor,' they chorused.

'Good morning,' said Graham.

'You may sit,' she said and her gaze surveyed the room slowly as they did, 'Sit up straight, Carlo. Patrizia! If I see a magazine on your desk again, I will confiscate!'

'*Scuse, Signora,*' said a small pretty girl as she stood up.

'In English!' she roared.

'Sorry, Miss.'

'I am sorry, Miss.!'

'I am sorry, Miss,' echoed Patrizia.

'Please excuse me,' roared her teacher.

'Please excuse me.'

'MISS!'

'Please excuse me, Miss.'
'Sit!'
Patrizia sat.

Signora Ferrara indicated a chair behind her desk, 'You may sit there, Doctor. I shall stand.'

Graham took the seat, facing the class. He felt a shiver run up his spine. A bully? No, a martinet, yes that's the word, he thought. She brought back terrifying memories of his fierce junior school teacher, Mrs Mount, and how at aged nine he had wet himself in sheer terror when wrongly accused of flicking ink pellets at another boy's white shirt, an event he had never lived down. Then his revelation of the true culprit's name had resulted in a subsequent beating in the playground.

Signora Ferrara said, 'Now we shall revise the last lesson. The future tense. Repeat after me. I shall go. You will go. He will go. She will go. It will go. We shall go. One shall go. You will go. They will go …'

The class repeated at full volume. Graham looked down at the desk. Had Ferrara read his chapter on futurity? Had she noted his statement that there was no future tense in English? Did she understand the difference between tense and aspect? Did she not understand that 'shall' and 'will' were interchangeable according to context? Or that 'shall' was preferable in suggestions? Had she failed to note that the contracted forms, we'll and you'll avoided the problem?

Individuals were now being selected as she pointed.
'He!' she barked and pointed.
'He will go,' said a boy quietly.
'Louder!'
'He will go!' shouted the boy.
'We!' she pointed at poor Patrizia.
'We will go,' said Patrizia.

'Wrong!' she said, 'We must understand that Patrizia prefers to read about stupid pop stars and cheap cosmetics instead of listening to her teacher!'

The class instinctively tried to laugh.

'Again!'

'We shall go?' Patrizia said tentatively.

'Next. They!' She pointed again.

Graham was in turmoil. Part of him wanted to suggest that Patrizia was perfectly correct in most, even all, situations. More of him was frankly scared of Signora Mount ... Signora Ferrara. The poor girl looked tearful. He tried to smile encouragingly in her direction. Patrizia noticed and shuddered.

Graham was exhausted by the time they left the room. Signora Ferrara stood expectantly looking at him.

'Um, it was a very disciplined lesson, er, Mrs Ferrara. Yes, very good ... strong ... class discipline.' Graham reflected this was why he had always avoided the teacher training area. You had to comment directly to people on their performance.

'Perhaps a famous educator like you, rather yourself, could suggest improvement?' Her face showed that she thought it impossible.

Graham remembered one piece of Malcolm O'Reilly's unwelcome advice at the compulsory Monday afternoon staff meetings. He coughed nervously, 'Well, yes. Excellent lesson ... but given a visitor, in this case a native speaker visitor, there was an opportunity to make use of the situation. The class could have asked me questions.'

'With which structures?'

'Well, freely. They must know basic questions such as What Do you do? Where do you live?'

'I could not intrude upon you. We were studying the future tense not the present simple.'

Graham winced. He didn't dare point out that *will /shall* wasn't actually a tense.

'The questions could be inappropriate! Impolite. Intrusive. Insolent. Rude. Cheeky. Disrespectful.'

'Of course,' Graham wondered if she were a walking thesaurus. Then thought, tyrannosaurus more like.

'Also it was not in my lesson plan.'

'Yes, I'm sure you're quite right,' Graham remembered in contrast O'Reilly on the importance of the ability to adapt and extemporize, a category on the RSA. Cert. TEFL Lesson Observation check sheet. Not that adapting and extemporizing were generally part of Graham's lesson plans, though sometimes a word or structure might lead him onto an interesting and lengthy aside. He had never imagined he would be quoting O'Reilly.

Malcolm O'Reilly found a parking space for his Saab on Bournemouth's prestigious Westover Road. He had an appointment with his hairdresser, something he always looked forward to with pleasure on alternate Mondays, but first he had time to go to the bookshop.

He found the travel section, and leafed through the guide books on Rome. They would only have two days, and he would be fully engaged in the conference. Gloria would be unlikely to stray beyond the main tourist attractions. In fact, it was highly likely that full-day tours of the city would be available with pick-ups at major hotels. Yes, so the slim volume, *Ten Places You Must See in Rome* should suffice. He glanced up, *Ten Places You Must See in Luxembourg* was on the shelf above. The guide book series, which was lengthy, was perhaps stretching the definition of 'must see.' Certainly the attractions of The Grand Duchy (if there were any) bore no comparison to the Colosseum, The Roman Forum, The Pantheon, The Piazza Navona or The Spanish Steps.

'Excuse me,' he asked the young man with a bookshop badge, 'There appear to be no phrase books here.'

'They're in the Languages section ... just around the corner,' he replied.

With just four days left to their flight to Rome, the BBC Italian Language series *Avventura* was far more than they could possibly absorb, and in any case O'Reilly had found the BBC's efforts at language teaching remarkably misguided. They put way too much into each lesson.

He picked up the tiny green phrase book. It would have far more than they might need. The list of menu items was essential. With a shudder, O'Reilly remembered once ordering eel in error in Lyons. He had seen *anguille* and for some reason, possibly the strong aperitif, imagined it was in some way connected to *agneu*, lamb. His school French lessons had not gone far into culinary matters. He leafed through to fish dishes in Italian. *Anguille,* so eels were just the same in Italian as in French. Then lamb was *agnello*. Excellent. He would be able to avoid the disgusting snake-like creatures and basic French should aid his comprehension. With his imminent hairdressing appointment in mind, he flicked to 'At The Barber's.' He chuckled. Would one ever need the Italian for anti-scurf lotion (*una lozione antiforfora*), whatever that might be. Then 'with the parting on the right / left' (*con la riga a destra / sinistra'*). 'Brush it over the bald part' was simpler in Italian (*col riporto*: informal).

'Morning, Malcolm.'

O'Reilly swivelled around. Bernard Arnold.

'A very good morning to you, Bernard.'

'Not at work today?'

'I needed to pick up some items for my forthcoming trip to Italy.'

'A phrase book? I thought you were a language teacher,' said Bernard, 'Hadn't you thought about actually learning the language? Trouble with phrase books, they teach you to ask a question then you've got no chance of understanding the answer.'

'Most amusing. What brings you into town?' said O'Reilly.

O'Reilly had never trusted people with a permanent grin plastered across their faces, let alone a Bobby Charlton brush over, which Bernard must fondly imagine concealed his balding pate. How strange that he had just read (or even learned) *col riporto*. It had stuck in his mind. Not that his own silvery locks needed that instruction. He decided not to suggest to Bernard that it would be a useful expression if he were ever to visit Italy.

'Six textbooks short for a new class,' said Bernard, 'I'm the only one free to come down here.'

'I remember. You don't have a personal assistant,' said O'Reilly smugly, 'Or administration staff.'

'The class teacher's chosen that book by Donaldson. I didn't have enough copies in the store cupboard. I suppose Donaldson swims against the tide. When everyone else is interested in functional syllabuses, Donaldson goes for old-fashioned grammar with long and indigestible texts full of new vocabulary.'

As much as this coincided with O'Reilly's personal view of Donaldson's textbook, there is an etiquette about defending your own team members. O'Reilly felt compelled to disagree.

'Graham is erudite on grammar. Also while some functional areas make sense, such as 'making suggestions' or 'greetings,' others are fake titles on basic grammar units. The example that springs to mind is 'talking about the recent past ' which is simply a lesson on the present perfect with a silly novel name,' said O'Reilly.

'You haven't studied Applied Linguistics though, have you, Malcolm?' sneered Bernard.

'Not at all. Teaching skills and communication ability outweighs Chomsky in my humble opinion. Are you still trailing off to Portsmouth Polytechnic twice a week? Their Diploma in Applied Linguistics course seems more akin to day release than a university course to me.' O'Reilly watched Bernard's instant snarl forced into his usual ingratiating smile.

'Maybe, but this is 1977. Donaldson's book is designed to appeal to teachers who were used to plodding through traditional French or German textbooks in the state system. It's a piece of crap.'

O'Reilly bristled. 'I believe its popularity is spreading,' he said.

'Seems to be,' said Bernard, 'Christ knows why. Look at that lot,' he pointed to the adjacent shelf unit. Four shelves were filled with copies of *Intercourse*.

'A light lunch only,' said Francesca, , 'Your talk is at sixteen hundred, then we will try to catch the train around eighteen-thirty or earlier to Milano ... Milan. Of course, we will now go to Giovanni's.'

'Must we really eat from the menu from before 1492?' said Mario.

'I think yes,' said Francesca, 'But Graham enjoyed it last evening.'

'Er ...' said Graham, 'Well, I ... um, yes, it was very nice.'

Giovanni greeted them with open arms, and shook hands vigorously with Graham, then placed an arm heavily around his shoulder, and spoke in Italian to Francesca.

'He says he has never seen someone enjoy his olive oil soup so much. He has more for you.'

'Perhaps I might try something different today,' ventured Graham nervously. The memory of the night grumbled in his stomach.

'Of course. Do you like pasta?' Francesca watched his blank expression, 'Spaghetti? Macaroni?'

'We have Spaghetti Bolognese for the staff lunches at World English Centre,' said Graham, 'On Wednesdays.'

'We normally have a pasta dish before the main course. The special pasta course is from before 1492, *cavatelli* pasta with *cavoletti di Bruxelles*, with walnuts in a cream sauce,' said Francesca, that's Brussels sprouts with a pasta. *Cavatelli con cavoletti*. It is a clever word play by Giovanni. Then he will follow with river trout. I think it will be good.'

Mario intervened, 'But not with the novella. I think it is more a *lassativo* than a wine.'

'Laxative,' interjected Francesca.

'I normally have a light lunch,' started Graham, 'I'm not used to drinking at lunchtime either.' Especially not with the talk looming in three hours time, he thought.

'We are in Italy!' said Mario cheerfully, 'It is only white wine. Not strong. So, *Vernaccia di San Gimignano*,' said Mario decisively to their host. 'The *trota* ... '

'Trout,' said Francesca.

'You see?' said Mario, 'She always corrects. So, the trout is too typical for *il Medioevo* ...'

'The Middle Ages,' said Francesca.

'What she said. The religious ...'

'Monks.'

'The monks must to eat the fish on holy days. Days when they cannot eat meat.'

'Fast days.'

'Thank you,' said Mario, glaring at Francesca, 'I think that Graham understands my meaning well. There were many fast days. Not only Friday, but many more saints' days. So all the *monastero* and *convento*...'

'Monasteries. And convents.'

'Monasteries,' he continued, 'had the lake ...'

'Pond,' said Francesca.

'The lake for the fish on fasting days. Normally the trout. It is too typical.'

'Very typical,' said Francesca, 'Excuse me. I must wash my hands.'

Mario watched her go, 'You see, Graham, we are all at NIE too frighten to speak the English before Francesca. She always tells us better. And I have the degree in History and English.'

'I could understand you very well,' said Graham. Yet again he was recalling O'Reilly. Confirm by smiling and nodding when students get it right. If they get it wrong, don't correct them. Just stop confirming and they'll often self-correct. Maybe the pompous fellow had had a point.

Francesca walked elegantly back to the table and took her seat. She looked around the busy restaurant. There was a baby in a high chair at a nearby table with a toddler sister in the next chair. The mess was extraordinary. A waiter was praising the children extravagantly, in spite of the screaming as the older one took the dessert away from the baby and started scoffing it with both her hands. The waiter immediately ran to the dessert trolley and brought another one. The parents and grandparents at the table were smiling and laughing at the antics. There were children at several tables and it was noisy.

'I will say one negative about my country. We are far too indulgent with children,' said Francesca, 'We do not draw the line and we tolerate too much the bad behaviour in restaurants.'

'You do not have children,' said Mario.

'I am not married,' said Francesca, 'And do not wish to be so. You will see children sleeping at tables at 10 p.m. It will not happen in Switzerland or Germany.'

'I think these children are charming,' said Mario indicating the baby and toddler, 'So sweet. I love the children.'

'All Italians will say this,' said Francesca, 'Especially the men who do nothing to feed and clean. But not me.'

. . .

Graham was feeling comfortable and replete. The sprouts had been a potential concern, combined with the after effects of the olive oil soup the day before, but the pasta and cream were proving to be a comfort food. He had to admit that Italian cuisine was proving far better than he had ever imagined. The trout was excellent. The dessert was a repeat of the evening before. He realised he was also feeling profoundly sleepy.

Graham sipped the espresso. It was incredibly strong, making him feel instantly livelier, 'I need to make some notes,' he said. 'I'm curious about the switching of town names ... for example you say Florence, but Mario and Giovanni say Firenze, even when speaking an English sentence. Then Naples and Napoli, and Milan and Milano.'

'It is a good question,' said Francesca, 'When should we translate and when not? It will differ.'

Mario intervened, 'The history is my interest. Italy is only a nation since eighteen-seventy. Italian cities were independence.'

'Independent states,' corrected Francesca.

Mario sighed, 'Yes. Then English has olden days names for the old capital cities ... Turin for Torino, Venice for Venezia, Genoa for Genova, Padua for Padova, Rome for Roma and as you say, Napoli for Naples.'

'Naples for Napoli,' she said.

'This was my meaning. As I think you are knowing,' said Mario.

Graham had his notebook and pen in hand.

'Then English adds an A for Apulia for Puglia, but extracts an A from Amalfi for Malfi,' added Francesca, 'As in the drama *The Duchess of Malfi.*'

'Shakespeare,' said Graham, 'Yes.'

'No, no, it is by Webster,' said Francesca.

Graham realized she was likely to be right. How annoying!

Mario exhaled, 'You can correct Dr Donaldson?' he said incredulously, 'This is too very much confident.'

'I correct because I am correct,' said Francesca, 'John Webster. First performance sixteen-thirteen, I believe?'

Graham nodded, 'She is right. My error.' He had no idea of the date of the wretched play. Nor anything about it whatsoever except vague recall of the title. His mind flicked to language ... *my error, my mistake, my fault?* No, not quite. *My fault* would indicate that the speaker had initiated the problem. Then there was the Latin, *mea culpa.* Somewhat pretentious. He wrote them in his notebook.

'Then Siracusa in Sicily is Syracuse in English. It is in *The Comedy of Errors,* but as Syracusa, as you will know, Graham,' she turned to Mario, 'That is by Shakespeare.'

Mario shrugged, 'Syracuse is also in *The Menaechmi* by Plautus, who has given Shakespeare the story.' He smiled at her victoriously, 'And in *A Winter's Tale,* Shakespeare was saying Sicilia, not Sicily.'

'However, it is *The Merchant of Venice,* not Venezia. Also *Two Gentlemen of Verona.'*

Mario smiled in triumph, 'Because there is no English translation of Verona.'

Graham observed their bickering and blatant attempts at ... what was the word? Yes, one-upmanship. Not a word he'd ever taught. That Grant fellow at WEC had warned him that English Literature was taught at the expense of English Language in Italy. Grant was correct, it would appear. Were they showing off for his benefit? Rather a waste of time. Graham was also unfamiliar with *A Winter's Tale.* While he felt qualified to give a detailed talk on the development of grammar and vocabulary from Chaucer to Shakespeare to the Restoration, he had always eschewed the actual plays on stage. He left that sort of theatrical nonsense to O'Reilly and his interminable plays for students at WEC. O'Reilly had been casting the annual pantomime for host families just before Graham left for Italy. Well, O'Reilly knew better than to ask him to dress up in silly costumes and prance about on a stage with ludicrous and vulgar dialogue in *Jack & The Beanstalk.* Graham chuckled to himself. O'Reilly had had the temerity in the summer to suggest that he, Graham Donaldson, might play a pathetic parson in *The Importance of Being Earnest*. He was third choice after two teachers had cried off with flu. He had certainly put him in his place. Graham looked at his companions. Their discussion was continuing.

'Some cities I would argue,' Francesca continued, 'English teachers in Livorno always call it Leghorn, but I think few native speakers know this, from the Battle of Leghorn.'

'Sixteen fifty-three,' said Mario quickly.

Graham was writing, 'So we have adjectives also: Genovese, Milanese, Venetian, Neapolitan. This is most interesting.'

'Also Roman,' said Mario.

'That is very obvious,' snapped Francesca.

Mario smiled, 'But football changes this. Perhaps you do not know this, Francesca.'

'In which way?' said Francesca.

'The football team is A.C. Milan, not Milano. This is because The English started the team as "Milan Football and Cricket Club." So it is always the English word, except in the Mussolini time. I am a fan.'

Francesca was glowering.

'Then I think ... no, I know certain ... English newspapers say Roma, Torino, Fiorentina and Napoli when they talk of the football.'

'Football, not "the" football,' said Francesca.

Mario said something fast in Italian, and she blushed.

'This was not polite to a lady,' she told Graham.

Graham drifted again as Francesca and Mario argued about the bill in Italian. From the volatility of the language and of the gestures he worked out that UUP were supposed to be paying but that Francesca thought that NIE might pay for Mario's more expensive choice of wine, of which Mario had consumed more than half. He watched

Mario reluctantly add some banknotes to the tray. Giovanni whipped the tray away, and returned with two carrier bags, one British Airways, one Alitalia. He started explaining something. Francesca nodded, then turned to Graham.

'Giovanni is making you a gift. This is olive oil,' she took out an unlabelled dark green glass wine bottle from the blue and red British Airways bag. It had a cork protruding slightly from it. 'The same olive oil as last night. It is precious, the best in Tuscany, which means the best in all Italy and so the world. It is from Montecarlo ... not the place in France, but a small Tuscan town near Lucca. This oil has won many awards. Giovanni purchases it in the barrel, and has filled a bottle for you and corked it.'

'But ... but,' started Graham in some alarm, 'Won't I have to carry it all the way round Italy with me?'

'Yes, and therefore you must be careful. Do not put in your suitcase.'

Graham looked at the other bag, 'I really shan't need two bottles.'

'No. I will take this one. The one in the green Alitalia bag. This is for Giovanni's friend in Napoli. He says they compete over the best olive oil and this year Tuscany can only be the victor. We will deliver it to his restaurant.'

Barry Grant hurried into the staff dining room at WEC. He'd finally managed to get away from the persistent questions of a Swiss-German ski instructor in I 14, his intermediate class. How was he supposed to know the English for items of ski equipment? He got his meal, shepherd's pie with peas, and saw Malcolm O'Reilly beckoning him. He sighed to himself. Malcolm had finished his lunch and was sipping a coffee. Malcolm always arrived in the staff dining room before the bell went for break so as to be the first to be served. Barry would have to join him, and inevitably Malcolm would light his post-luncheon Passing Clouds cigarette, which would flavour Barry's lunch. Barry put his tray down on Malcolm's table.

'Do join me, Barry,' Malcolm O'Reilly patted the chair next to him.

Barry sat, 'Thank you, Malcolm.'

'I wanted to thank you for assisting Donaldson. It must have been a chore.'

'Not really,' said Barry, 'I told him about the Italian secondary school system, and he barely listened to a word that I said. He said the book was for private language schools.'

Malcolm tutted, 'Quite typical. No doubt his publishers will disabuse him, and explain that selling a book to a class of forty is more profitable than to a class of eight or ten. Why does he think they invited him to tour around speaking to secondary teachers? Not to put too fine a point upon it, the man is an ass. Do you mind if I smoke?'

'Not at all,' said Barry through clenched teeth.

'I smoke just the two a day. One after each meal,' said Malcolm.

'That's a very Italian habit,' said Barry, 'Gabriella's father does exactly the same.'

'How is Gabriella?'

'She's fine, thank you, Malcolm. The university has suggested she attend the Rome conference at the weekend, so you will see her there.'

'I was hoping as much,' said Malcolm, 'Such a sweet girl.'

'Yes,' said Barry, 'Um, would you mind if I bring up a trade union matter?' English language teachers had recently affiliated themselves to MATSA (Managerial, Administrative, Technical & Supervisory Association), a branch of the General & Municipal Workers trades union, and Barry had been elected union representative. They avoided the term shop steward as too factory based.

Malcolm frowned, 'Perhaps my office is more appropriate.'

'It won't take long. There's some discontent about the loss of free periods while Graham Donaldson is away. I've just been teaching his personal class, I 14.'

'I wondered why you were clutching his dreadful book,' said Malcolm.

'You spend the whole lesson explaining arcane vocabulary,' complained Barry, 'Today was the "The Origin of the Penny Post." It's not fascinating as a vehicle for contextualizing the passive voice though I have to admit the grammar is sound. Anyway, in the Intermediate Department, we've all lost free periods filling in for Graham. I know you've done one a day ... but on next Friday and Monday, we'll be covering your lesson too.'

Malcolm felt anger rising, 'I believe it has been said many times that they are not free periods. They are simply not time-tabled, and I believe you will find that your contracts cover six lessons a day, therefore thirty lessons per week. The fact that I decide to reduce that to twenty-five at normal times is irrelevant. I do so to allow for cover for illness.'

'I understand, but this absence was known some considerable time ago, and it all falls on one department. It's not like an office job where if you're away, the work just piles up on your desk. When a teacher's away, someone has to do the job instead. When they come back, the work's been done. And we've had to do it all from within the Intermediate department. Might the Elementary and Advanced departments not help out too?'

'I hardly imagine that Pamela would cope with the move up from Elementary level to people who can actually speak some English, and the students would no doubt find Llewellyn's erudite Advanced level lessons far beyond them.'

'Both examples are at the extreme,' said Barry, 'And isn't the point of Graham Donaldson's textbook that any teacher can follow it? So that students get a consistent syllabus rather than the teacher's choice on the day? That seems worthwhile to me.'

The afternoon talk was in a lecture hall at the university. Graham was gratified to see around two hundred teachers sitting patiently waiting for his talk. Over 95% of them were women too. It hadn't been so long ago that WEC had only employed male teachers. Five years? Six? Younger teachers like Grant had found the unusual Swiss policy sexist and protested against it. They had pointed out that language faculties in universities invariably had a female majority. Graham had considered that a fair point, and indeed many of the males employed were far from language specialists. Chancers on the prowl. Graham shuddered at the memory of that appalling ex-actor Roger Fleetwood. Ignorant fellows, too. Nevertheless, there had been a quality of relaxation about having only male colleagues, thought Graham. They were content not to speak to you for a start. He was happy to be totally ignored, left alone in his own world in his corner of the staff room. Women tended to expect a conversation between lessons. Much of it was irrelevant chatter, and also intrusive. Women tended to badger one with questions. On the other hand the female presence ameliorated the Neanderthal vulgarity and coarse comments that he remembered from the days when Grace-Pitleigh and Morgan had worked alongside him. Thank goodness both had departed. No one had joked in the staffroom about breaking wind before being trapped in the next lesson since they had left.

'This is Dr Rossi from the university who will be introducing you,' said Francesca.

'What?' Graham's mind had drifted away from the here and now. He looked at the man. In his sixties. Brown suit. Green woollen knitted waistcoat. Tie. Balding head at the front, long and grey hair at the back.

'Dr Rossi, said the man, 'I am delighted to meet you. How are you enjoying the wonderful sights of our city?'

Francesca intervened, 'We have had no time, sadly.'

'Not even the Ponte Vecchio? Not the Palazzo Medici, the Piazza della Signoria or the Duomo?' asked Rossi, 'That is a tragedy rather than a pity.' He turned to Graham, 'If you have time, I should be delighted to accompany you. We could at least take coffee together in the Piazza. It is ridiculously overpriced in one manner, yet in another it is worth every lira for the sights. '

Graham pondered, did they mean sites, as in ancient sites, or sights as in something to look at? Fascinating. It must go in his notebook.

Francesca spoke, 'Dr Donaldson only arrived yesterday evening, and we are departing for Milan immediately after the talk,' she said.

Dr Rossi shook his head sadly, 'To come to Florence without seeing David,' he said.

Graham wondered who this David fellow was.

Dr Rossi's introduction had been long, fulsome and switched between Italian and English. For a second, Graham had been surprised to find the entire audience were professors, then remembered his colleague Grant's comment that *professore* meant teacher rather than the head of a university department. Apparently Americans also used 'professor' over-widely. The talk had gone better than any Graham had ever given. Never had he experienced such serious and concentrated attention.

Dr Rossi came and shook hands at the end, 'I hope you will come back so that I can introduce you to David,' he said.

Graham shrank back. Was the man a homosexual, talking about his partner? He needed to acknowledge the introduction though. 'Thank you for your kind words. I must congratulate you on your English.'

The man looked perplexed, 'I'm sorry?' he said.

'You speak English very well, Dr Rossi,' said Graham. To himself he thought, well, apart from all those intrusive final vowels ... *i-fa you have-a time-a.*

'My name is Ross. Not Rossi. Dr Ross. I'm from Cheltenham ... that is to say I am English.'

'English?' said Graham in surprise.

The man looked downcast, 'I have been teaching here for thirty years. Since 1947. My wife is Italian, and I always speak Italian at home. Have I acquired an Italian accent then?'

'Um. Somewhat. Final vowel sounds,' murmured Graham, 'That's why I thought ... er, that Miss Garibaldi had said Rossi.' He reflected, and she adds a slight final vowel sound on words too. How embarrassing.

'I had no idea,' said Dr Ross, 'I suppose I adopted an accent because my students found it easier to understand me. I had never realized. Oh, dear ... oh, dear.'

Mario pointed out the pink, green and white of the Duomo at least on the way to the railway station.

'I'm so sorry that you upset, Dr Ross about his accent,' said Francesca, 'He has written significant texts on linguistics and is an expert on pronunciation. He seemed quite distraught.'

Graham decided against mentioning that she herself had originally added that intrusive and confusing final vowel *Rossi*. She had just done so again. Why make a fuss? After all he was in the woman's hands for a week. At her mercy. In her power. Subject to her will. He should not have put his notebook in his briefcase. Now he would need to remember later.

Mario dropped them on the taxi rank, ignoring the calls and vigorously aggressive gestures of the taxi drivers. Graham took his bags and turned towards the station entrance.

'You should thank, Mario,' hissed Francesca, 'We won't be seeing him again.'

'Er, ah … yes, thank you, um, Mario,' Graham managed.

'Thank you, Dr Donaldson … wait! You have left your olive oil in the car.' Mario handed him the bag. Francesca was holding hers already.

'I must get the tickets,' she said, 'You should stand here and guard our bags.'

Graham looked at a large crowd of people pushing and shoving each other to his left.

'The ticket office,' explained Francesca, 'We do not queue in an orderly fashion like the British.' Francesca plunged into the crowd, arms tight against her sides, and started to wriggle and elbow her way forward through the struggling mass.

Graham realized he would have stood no chance of obtaining a ticket. It took Francesca ten minutes, but that was remarkably faster than others in the scuffling melee. Fracas. Scrum. Free-for-all. Rough and tumble. Virtually a brawl. Well, they could be noted on the train.

'We must hurry,' she said, 'This way … we are lucky. We can just make the TEE in time. It's faster.'

Graham stumbled along after her. The train towered over them. There was no platform. How extraordinary. What did the woman mean talking about tea? She was at the carriage steps, 'Come! Be careful your bag!'

Graham clambered up the steps with suitcase in one hand, briefcase and British Airways bag in the other. The door slammed behind him, and he nearly fell over as the train jerked forward. He was standing in a corridor next to full compartments. The corridor was packed with standing people.

'There are no seats,' said Francesca, 'But it is only two hours. A very fast train ... TEE, Trans Europe Express. I had hoped for the earlier one, but Mario was driving too cautiously.'

That comment shocked Graham, who had been terrified of their speed weaving through heavy traffic.

'It is good,' she continued, 'For we are meeting Signor Martini at nine ... he is the director of NIE and in a way, my boss too.' She glanced at her watch, 'We will have no time to wash and change. But you can leave your bags at the hotel. They will place them in your room. I can leave mine with the porter also until later. It is a good hotel. It will be secure, I hope, but do keep your wallet on your person,' she opened her handbag and took out a pocket mirror, 'I hope I will have time to freshen my make-up. Signor Martini is a very ...' she searched for the word, 'Fastidious person. It is a very expensive and prestigious restaurant. It is near your hotel.'

The train was hot. Graham felt sticky and sweaty. A man in grey uniform was pushing towards them. Francesca explained, 'The ticket inspector. Take our tickets, please. I will not speak. Often these people are afraid to speak English, so it will be best if you deal with him. Perhaps then he will leave us alone.'

The inspector squeezed through the crowd, '*Biglietto*,' he demanded.

'Sorry. I don't speak Italian,' said Graham.

'Madonna!' muttered the inspector in irritation, 'Ticket. Please.'

Graham handed them over.

'Supplement charge,' said the inspector.

'What?'

'Supplement charge. For the sitting.'

'I'm not sitting,' said Graham, 'I'm standing.' Was the fellow an idiot?

'TEE all sitting train. Supplement for sitting.'

'What?' Graham looked pleadingly at Francesca.

'I don't speak Italian,' she said, 'Please. We don't understand.'

The inspector looked down at her suitcase, 'You not speaking Italian, Signora Garibaldi?'

'Signorina,' she snapped automatically, then sighed and switched to Italian. The tickets were stamped. Banknotes were proffered and put in the inspector's leather bag.

The inspector pushed his way on. Graham heard him demand, '*Supplemento*,' to the next person, then on down the train.

'What was that about?' he asked.

'On this special TEE train there is a supplementary seat charge,' she explained.

'There are no seats.'

'There seldom are at this time of evening. But you may not board the train without a seat.'

'So why is everyone standing?'

'If they did not allow this, people would not be able to travel. This is Italy. It is a practical solution. But they will demand the seat charge also. This is also typical of Italy. I was hoping to avoid this.'

Milano Centrale. It was massive. Graham stared around open-mouthed.

'This railway station is a famous building. Rebuilt by Mussolini in 1931. It is like a monument to Fascism.'

'Mussolini made the trains run on time?' ventured Graham. He had heard that often. He snickered, 'But with a supplementary charge, no doubt.'

'He did. Also he built the *autostrada*. This building is bigger than the normal human ...' she searched for the word.

'Scale. It is out of scale,' said Graham.

'Ah. I learn something new today. Like the machine for weighing, or on a fish?'

'Yes, yes,' said Graham, nodding as the topic started to interest him. There was the verb, perhaps to scale a wall, or rather a mountain or cliff. A social scale. A pay scale. A scale model. A widescale problem. A timescale. The earthquake was ... well, whatever it was ... on the Richter scale. The Beaufort scale for winds. Fascinating, then of course a scale in music. Or of music? Ah! Limescale. Were there any more? Dentists! They scaled teeth, not that Graham had ever experienced it, but the women teachers had been discussing it at WEC the week before. This was exciting ... another! The scales fell from his eyes. Literary rather than everyday speech though. Expressions ... yes, to tip the scales. Off the scale. On a grand scale ...

Francesca noticed that his eyes had glazed over yet again, 'You can see the same in Germany. They created buildings for giants. This was their idea. To make people feel small.'

'To dwarf people,' said Graham, 'They scaled up the size of the buildings.' Where was his notebook when he needed it? He had missed that one.

'Exactly. Thank you. Please remember also, that Mussolini was executed by Italian partisans,' she stressed 'Italian', 'This happened in a town nearby, and the body was brought to Milan and displayed near this station. It was abused by the public. Kicked, urinated upon, then hanged by the feet.'

Graham tried to imagine the grisly image. Then tried to forget it.

'Now. We must stand close together,' said Francesca, 'We will hold our bags on our inside between us, and link arms also to walk.'

Graham had never liked touching other people, 'Why?'

'You will see. Beggars. Vagabonds. Drug addicts. Thieves. There are many police in here, but someone can take a bag and run.'

The long steps down gave Graham vertigo, and for just a moment he was glad Francesca was holding his arm tightly.

All down the steps, youths were sitting at the edges. His eyes bulged as he watched one roll up his sleeve and start injecting himself. He looked down and stepped past a discarded syringe. A strange fruity smoke hung in the air, 'Sodom and Gomorrah,' he said.

'More or less,' said Francesca, 'The police prefer to keep it all in one place where they can supervise and observe. It is better than all over the city. Now we may have difficulty with a taxi because ... well, we may be lucky.'

They walked out into a light drizzle. Francesca marched to the first taxi, and spoke. The driver was shaking his finger at her. She tried the one behind, then came back.

'Bastards. They won't carry us because the distance is so short to the hotel. The first one said he had waited fifteen minutes to get to the front of the taxi line. I offered more money and told him that it was raining, but he was not interested. So, we must walk. This has happened before. I wonder why the office always books this hotel.'

Graham trailed after her through the rain. The suitcase felt heavier with every step, then there was the briefcase and the bag with the olive oil in the other hand. The hotel was only a few hundred yards away. Francesca checked him in, and Graham handed over his passport.

'Do you wish to use the Gentlemen in the lobby?' she said, 'The restaurant is close, but we are already a little late.'

Graham shook his head. After the events of the night, his normal costive state had returned. He felt sealed.

'Perhaps you would wait for me then?' she said, 'I must check my make-up.'

They were led through a busy restaurant to double obscured glass doors with an ornate pattern etched into them. A private dining room. The waiter thrust open the doors. An imposing rather plump man stood up. He was wearing a pale blue suit and a beautiful silk tie. His silver hair was immaculate. A waft of pungent after-shave filled the air. He immediately reminded Graham strongly of Malcolm O'Reilly. This one seemed even smarter, and even vainer too.

'Doctor Donaldson. It is a great pleasure to meet you in person. I am Martini.'

Graham snuffled, 'Martini … Garibaldi … is everyone in Italy named after food or drink?'

There was absolute silence as his listeners drank in the comment. Francesca broke the ice, 'And you are named Graham. Americans, I believe, call some of their biscuits Graham crackers. Would you like the name Graham Crackers?'

Signor Martini laughed and patted Graham's shoulder, 'Francesca is a very clever girl with a sense of humour. Please sit next to me. You really must excuse my poor English.' Graham was aware that not only was Signor Martini's English accent excellent, but also that Martini knew that.

The door opened. They looked up. Graham was shocked at the apparition. The girl had spiky hair with blue and pink streaks. She was wearing a leopard print mini skirt over fishnet tights and heavy black boots. Her torn denim jacket was open to reveal a T-shirt with a ragged neck and the wording 'Anarchy in the UK.' Graham stared at the silver nose stud.

'Sorry, I'm late. There was a queue in the bogs.'

'This is Luciana, my assistant,' said Francesca.

'I have ordered,' said Signor Martini, 'You must be relieved to be in Milan after all that Tuscan peasant food. The food in Tuscany is wholesome, and …'

'Hearty,' suggested Francesca.

'I bow to your knowledge of English,' he said, 'But it is not sophisticated. We will commence with *risotto alla Milanese*. This is arborio rice with chicken stock, butter and a great quantity of saffron. It will have seasonal shavings of white truffle. It is typical of Lombardy. Then I have ordered *ossobuco*. You must know it?'

'I'm afraid not,' said Graham.

'Veal shanks? Yes, shanks, with bone marrow, cooked with vegetables and white wine. This restaurant will cook the traditional one without tomatoes. We will serve it with polenta and a Barbera wine, I think. For dessert, we will have English soup ...' he laughed loudly at Graham's expression, 'My joke. We call it *Zuppa Inglese* ... you would call it sherry trifle. You need a good rich meal for your journey goes next to the South, where unfortunately you must subsist on raw vegetables, oil and fish. You will see. The people in the far south are not true Italians, but rather more Greek, or even Arab.'

After the first course, Signor Martini left the room to 'wash his hands.' Francesca turned to Luciana, 'What are you wearing, Luciana? Signor Martini is the head of the company. This occasion is not a punk rock concert! Also, you are twenty-six, not seventeen.'

'Oh, he won't mind, Cesca. Nah, he'll be pleased. Everyone will think he's picked up a young mistress. He'll be right flattered. Any road, this is Milan. They're totally into fashion. I made an effort. I took out me safety pin and stuck with just the silver stud,' she pointed to her nose.

Her accent was Northern English. Graham was perplexed, 'Are you from Manchester?' he said sharply.

'Nah. Blackpool. Me full name's Luciana Ramsbotham. Don't comment. I've heard it. Sheep's bum at school. Me mum's Italian. Me dad's English. I were born in Blackpool.'

'You're over-doing the accent,' said Francesca waspishly.

Luciana grinned, 'Fair enough,' she turned to Graham, 'They run a trattoria just off the Golden Mile. Steak and Trat. Fake Italian cuisine for the totally pissed punter. Pizza with decent cheddar cheese instead of the mucky sticky mozzarella shit.'

Francesca shook her head, 'Well, that costume won't do at all when we're in the South. Wear a dress, please. Luciana will be travelling and organising our display stand in Rome at the weekend,' she explained.

'South?' said Graham, 'I thought Rome was the middle.'

'No, no,' said Francesca, 'Believe me. Rome is the South. Florence and Bologna is the middle.'

Signor Martini returned and took his seat, and he put on an ingratiating smile, 'So Luciana, I am most interested in this *Never Mind The Bollocks It's The Sex Pistols*. It appears to be an anarchic and powerful statement of the youth.' He patted her fishnet clad knee.

'You've heard it?' said Luciana incredulously as she moved his hand away.

'Oh, yes. *Anarchy in the UK. Holidays in The Sun. God Save The Queen*, of course. Though in many ways I prefer The Pink Floyd or Supertramp. Please tell me more,' he turned, 'I'm sure Dr Donaldson knows The Pink Floyd.'

'The Punk Who?' said Graham.

'Of course, as an intellectual, I am personally a socialist,' said Martini, 'So I have sympathy with these punk bands. *White Riot* by The Clash is a favourite.'

'Fuck me!' said Luciana.

6 / MILANO

Francesca looked around the table. Graham Donaldson was struggling to keep his eyes open, and his head kept dropping to his chest, then he'd start awake with a snort and a shudder. Signor Martini was leaning too far forward desperately trying to appear relevant and cool to an increasingly wary Luciana. Francesca was fully aware that any knowledge Martini might have gleaned about punk music was taken from observing his daughters' purchases ...he had two, aged fifteen and seventeen. The order of glasses of Glenfiddich had been the final straw for poor Graham, who had already seemed extremely tired and drowsy before the meal had even started.

Then she had the surprise news from Martini to digest. So UUP were sending out Graham's editor, and she would be stuck with him for the rest of the week. He was due to arrive tomorrow late morning. Martini had warned her to be most careful to make sure he paid his way. She had past experience of editors expecting marketing to pick up their bills. Martini had advised that she simply kept a list of everything she paid for, which she should submit to the editorial department at the end. However, an editor on a straightforward author tour was a novel event.

Martini's antics were becoming embarrassing. Time to make a move.

'Thank you for a wonderful dinner, Signor Martini, but I'm afraid Dr Donaldson has had a long and tiring day. I should take him back to his hotel now,' she noted Graham's audible sigh of relief, 'I will be taking a taxi to my apartment from the hotel, so I can drop you on the way, Luciana.'

'Are you sure? Let me order more whisky. You don't need to go yet, Luciana ...' he pleaded in a slurred voice.

'I have details of the itinerary which I must check with Luciana,' said Francesca firmly, 'She will need to meet Signor Winthrop at the airport.' She stood up, 'So, *Andiamo.*'

Graham felt more than slightly dizzy with sleepiness. The short walk back in the cold night air had only partly woken him, though Luciana's pithy comments on Signor Martini had cut through the haze. He had never heard a woman use such words. Then again he didn't know any women apart from the staff at WEC. After Luciana had made a few coarse remarks to Francesca, they had both switched to Italian, which had spared him unwanted information. At least the hotel was modern and anodyne. He had asked for an eight o'clock alarm call, and when told about the bedside radio-alarm had protested that he could never work the stupid things. It was certainly not worth unpacking as they were off in the morning at ten. He stared at the desk. There was that blessed red and blue British Airways bag with the olive oil. They had placed it directly opposite the bed. No bath though. A shower with a drain hole in the tiled floor.

He took off his shoes. What had Martini been saying? Giles Winthrop was flying in to join him for the tour tomorrow? It might be a relief to have an English person with him among all these vastly over-talkative Italians, though in their favour, they certainly seemed to know how to eat well. Today's dinner had been as superb as the evening before. Then Winthrop could hold his own in a conversation on grammar too, and would defer to Graham's decisions. So why in Heaven's name was the fellow coming?

'Three talks!' said Graham in alarm.

'Yes. Eleven, two thirty, then four thirty,' said Francesca. 'NIE have permission for state teachers to take time off to attend. Then we must cater for the private language schools, some of which are in nearby towns such as Monza, and also for tertiary education. In this way we will have the maximum audience. Only an hour for each talk.'

'I had assumed I would be speaking only the once,' complained Graham.

'You spoke twice yesterday. It is repeating the same talk,' she said, 'And today they will all come to you,' she waved her arm to show the state-of-the-art lecture room in NIE's headquarters building. It was steeply raked with comfortable seating and gleaming blonde wood. 'Also, you will have enough time for a pleasant lunch. Fortunately, as we are flying to Bari this evening.' Francesca looked at her watch, 'I'm afraid poor Mr Winthrop will probably arrive too late for lunch, but hopefully he can attend the afternoon sessions.'

'Due to the heavy rain, please disembark a few at a time and wait until we signal you,' the air steward put down his microphone.

Giles Winthrop was seated in the second row from the back of the Boeing 757. To his deep annoyance it had been the only seat available due to the late booking and then his late arrival at Heathrow, so he was in the smoking section. His suit would reek for a week. Not only that, the queue for the toilet had been right by his aisle seat, so he had spent much of the flight in close proximity to queuing bottoms. He had waved the unappetizing plastic food tray away when it was brought around. Breakfast? A lukewarm sausage and a lump of tepid scrambled egg with a plastic beaker of long-life orange juice. He couldn't face it, and wished he'd at least had a croissant at Heathrow. Not that there'd been any time. The rain was lashing the outside of the cabin windows. Everyone was pulling bags from the overhead storage bays and pushing to the front. Giles stood and allowed the two plump Italian ladies to exit into the aisle. Everyone was pushing forward.

'Due to the heavy rain, please disembark a few at a time and wait until we signal you,' came the announcement again.

It had been a surprise on Monday morning, when he had been summoned to James's office and handed the ticket. He resented the managing director's offhand comment that as he was a bachelor, it would be no issue for him to depart at once to Italy for six days. Not that he had much planned, and when he complained, James had immediately offered to pay cash for his concert recital ticket for the Friday evening and had said that he would go in his place. That was almost certainly a polite lie. Giles doubted that James had any enthusiasm for Bartok.

Giles wondered why everyone was in such an agitated and impatient hurry to disembark. Passport control followed by the wait in the baggage hall would eliminate any time advantage. He found himself the last in line as he edged along to the exit at the front. He looked down at the crowd in torrential rain virtually fighting to get onto the articulated bus, parked a hundred metres from the plane steps. A second bus was trundling through puddles on the tarmac towards them.

'Happens every time,' said the steward, 'They all rush off and stand there getting soaked. It's always two bus-loads, but none of them will wait for the second bus,' he looked at Giles, 'If I were you, I'd stay here and wait. It won't leave without the cabin crew anyway.'

'I was intending to,' said Giles, 'What extraordinary behaviour.'
'Ah. Is this your first visit to Italy then?' said the steward.

'I have much to check before the afternoon,' Francesca had said,
'Fortunately, Signora Ricci from NIE's design department speaks
excellent English, and she has offered to accompany you.'

The woman was small, and buxom ... a word Graham had not
used before, with long black curly ringlets descending over her
shoulders, and gleaming peacock blue eye make-up, 'Please. You must
call me Fiorella. It is the Italian for flower,' said the woman. She was
simpering. Graham wondered if she was seeking some gallant remark
on her floral Christian name. That was certainly not his style.

To his horror, she linked arms with him as they set off to the
restaurant.

'The salami antipasti is famous in this restaurant,' she said, 'You are
busy this afternoon, so this will be light, *cotoletta alla Milanese,* this is
milk-fed veal ... do you know the Austrian *wiener schnitzel?* No?
This is similar, though not exactly the same. We cook in much butter.
For many years, Lombardia ... Lombardy ... was part of the Hapsburg
Empire, and in 1859 ...'

Graham's mind wandered. Did these people only ever discuss
food and their convoluted history? It would seem so. Five minutes
later, he was wishing the topic had remained on food and history.
The woman had taken off her jacket, and her blouse was virtually
transparent, revealing lacy underwear which was failing to conceal
her cleavage.

'So are you married, Graham?' she had started.
'Er, no, I am a bachelor,' what an intrusive question!
'Ah. You play the field, I think you say. You are the Playboy!'
'Not at all.'

'My husband is businessman. He is always travelling. Hong Kong. New York. Parigi ... Paris. I do not trust him. When he returns he is always tired,' she lowered her eyes coquettishly, 'You understand.'

'Jet lag?' enquired Graham.

'Maybe this too. I mean he is too tired to be, how would you say, interested?'

'Ah. You mean he is dull ... not interesting,' the interesting / interested confusion was well-covered in *Intercourse*. Graham brightened. His explanation of the issue had long been a favourite part of his lessons.

'No, no, I know this difference, like amused and amusing. Surprised and surprising. My English teacher in Monza explained this well. I mean he is not interested in me.'

Graham was shocked. Well, it was shocking. The woman expected him to act as some kind of therapist or confidante, 'I see. He doesn't listen.'

'This too. I mean he is not interested in me as a woman,' she paused, 'I mean sex.'

Graham choked on his salami. He had always walked away from men who were conversing on that subject. He had never expected a female to introduce it in conversation.

'And when he does. It is ...' she paused again, 'I don't want to embarrass you, I see you are red in your face. Is this embarrassing for you? Well, it is in and out. Two minutes start to finish. He takes no time. Yes, I see you are embarrassed.'

'Excellent. Excellent. The correct distinction between embarrassing and embarrassed. Your teacher taught this very well ...' said Graham desperately, 'Veal? I haven't had it for a long time.'

'Nor me. This is what I am saying.'

'Did Luciana help you arrange your plane tickets for the rest of the week?' asked Francesca.

'Yes, we did it at the airport,' said Giles. In retrospect it was annoying that Luciana had then hurried him straight out to a taxi on the grounds that she needed to get back to help. He hadn't realized he would miss lunch entirely, and a coffee and sandwich would have been welcome, even in an airport café. 'Luciana was surprised they took my Access card.'

'In Italy many or rather most establishments still prefer cash payments,' said Francesca, 'This week I shall be carrying quite a frightening amount of cash for hotels and restaurants,' she stared at him, 'I do not quite understand the purpose of your journey.'

'Each editor is being assigned one of more European countries for special interest, as our ELT sales are increasing so rapidly. I was assigned Italy.'

'Yet you do not speak Italian,' stated Francesca.

'This is my first visit ever. It seemed bizarre to me. I studied French, Latin and Classical Greek at school, but, well, France and Greece were chosen by more senior editors so ...'

'You were left with Italy,' she laughed, 'Well, the Rome conference takes place at the edge of the Vatican City so you may be able to use your Latin. Also our sales are greater than either France or Greece.'

'I have enrolled for Italian evening classes from January,' said Giles quickly. Francesca did not seem impressed. 'Also, there's something I need to talk to Donaldson about, and I'm rather hoping you will be of help.'

When Graham arrived back in the lecture room. Luciana was putting leaflets on chairs, and Giles Winthrop was at the front talking to Francesca. Luciana was wearing a plain black dress, but the spikey hair and silver nose stud still stood out. The boots looked even more incongruous with a dress.

'Winthrop,' said Graham, nodding a terse greeting.

'Good afternoon, Graham,' said Giles, 'I trust you had a pleasant lunch.'

'The food was a good standard,' he said. He did not add that it had been a most unpleasant hour.

'I envy you. I haven't had a bite to eat all day. I must say, it seems so odd meeting up all this way from England,' said Giles.

'Yes.' Graham wondered if there were a distinction between 'meeting,' and 'meeting up.' He'd have to think about it.

Luciana came over, 'How was our lovely Fiorella?' she said.

'Um, well, er ...'

'Bend your ear, did she?' said Luciana, 'Husband's a right bastard. Tells everyone about him. She caught me on Monday, by the photocopier. Talk about explicit detail. There were things we've never heard of in Blackpool, and we're dirty weekend territory. I told her she needs to give him the elbow. I expect she will,' she looked round the room, 'That's the leaflets all done. I'll open up the doors and let the punters in.'

Graham stared out. Meeting up? Open up? Surely 'up' was quite redundant. Then his reaction to Fiorella. Her revelations were disgusting. He had been disgusted. He was sure that one was missing from the section on -ing / -ed words. How annoying. He was annoyed ... or irritated. It was irritating.

Graham and Giles sat on the hard plastic bucket seats in silence. Graham appreciated the absence of any idle chitter-chatter. The existing noise and clamour of Linate airport was quite enough.

'Olive oil?' said Giles eventually, pointing to the British Airways bag.

'Yes. More than a nuisance.'

'Miss Garibaldi has one too.'

'Yes.'

Giles yawned. It was not a surprise that getting conversation from Graham was like getting blood out of a stone, 'So the oil is hand baggage on the flight?'

'Yes.'

'I must say there was no warning of a strike when I arrived in Milan this morning,' said Giles, 'Still, strike disruption should make us feel as if we're at home.'

'Indeed.'

Giles saw Francesca pushing her way through the crowd towards them. He stood up at once. Francesca took the seat next to him gracefully, and Giles regained his seat. Graham had not moved.

Francesca exhaled, 'Well, the good news is that the flight to Bari has not been cancelled. The delay is only two hours therefore we should arrive at our hotel before midnight.'

'That's a relief,' said Giles.

'Then we have bad news too. Not only are the airport shops and cafés closed, but there will be no in-flight service. There is no catering to load onto the aircraft, which is combined with the ATI cabin crew refusing service in sympathy with the strikers.'

'Good lord!' snorted Graham, 'You mean that we will get nothing to eat whatsoever!'

'I'm afraid this is so.'

'Appalling,' Graham continued, 'I'm expected to deliver three ... three! ... three talks and cast adrift in a filthy airport with nothing to eat!'

Giles coughed, 'At least you had a decent lunch. I haven't eaten in twenty-four hours.'

'I missed lunch also,' said Francesca, 'Except for a small calzone and salad. And some panettone with an espresso. The food in the airport restaurant is merely average, but I had intended that we should at least have pasta, a small steak and some salad.'

The three sat glumly staring into space, imagining dining on pasta and a small steak.

'Peanuts!' said Giles suddenly, 'Salted peanuts!' The others stared at him. Graham recalled that starvation could lead to hallucinations. Not only were the shops closed, but the two vending machines had been emptied before they even got to the airport.

'James! Thank you, James!'

Graham shifted sideways with a shudder. The man had cracked.

'James ... the managing director of UUP! He remembered that Francesca was terribly fond of British KP nuts!'

'How thoughtful of him,' said Francesca, who was also beginning to doubt Giles' sanity. She recalled praising the tiny and greasy bowl proffered to her at a reception at UUP. Her praise had been entirely insincere, bordering on ironic.

'I'm so glad they didn't let us check our bags yet,' Giles was fumbling for his keys.

Graham pondered. Past simple tense with 'yet.' It made a degree of sense in the situation, yet from memory *Intercourse* stated categorically that 'yet' appeared with the present perfect tense, never with the past. He would need to check. There were several pages of revision notes for the next edition already.

Giles bent down and unlocked his bag, he scrabbled inside and emerged with an extra large blue and yellow pack of peanuts, 'Look! Food! He sent them for you. For you!'

Francesca held back the first thought, which was that the entire pack was rightfully hers then. 'We can share them,' she said, 'Of course.'

'There are no plates or bowls,' said Graham.

Giles felt a surge of nastiness bubbling up within him, 'If you'd rather not join us ... you did have lunch, after all. In a first class restaurant. Three courses, was it?'

'No, no. I am the one who has had to work all day delivering lectures,' said Graham, 'I simply meant that I am not in the habit of eating food from greasy packets in public places with my fingers.'

Francesca swallowed hard. Organizing three sets of teachers. Going around making sure she introduced herself to everyone. Having to listen to Graham's unending catalogue of minor complaints. She opened her handbag and took out a pack of paper handkerchiefs, 'We can have one each.'

They all sat in silence picking up peanuts from the paper hankies on their laps and eating them.

'They are extremely salty,' said Graham, 'Too salty. And I now realize that we have nothing whatsoever to drink afterwards either. I shall have to complain to your managing director about this.'

What an uncomfortable aeroplane it was. As it lurched and bumped alarmingly, Graham looked for the umpteenth time at the yellowing plastic-covered emergency card from the seat pocket. Douglas DC-9. This would be one to avoid in future. He knew nothing about aeroplanes, apart from the great British triumph of the Comet jet. He remembered that. Oh, and the Spitfire. The Ark Royal, the Comet, HMS Vanguard, The Flying Scotsman, the Morris Minor, the Mini. Donald Campbell and Bluebird. Perhaps that could form a unit if UUP commissioned the next level. British achievements. That should interest foreign learners. At least he had been spared more inane conversation. The three hours at the airport had been quite enough for one day, listening to Winthrop explaining the complexities of the British public school system to Garibaldi. She had found his description of fagging most amusing. The Garibaldi woman had shown some sense finally in saying that he must be exhausted and might prefer not to sit with her and Winthrop, as they would be having a business conversation.

A curt 'I don't speak Italian,' had fended off the hirsute Italian fellow next to him on the plane who had ventured to start a conversation. Graham closed his eyes.

· · ·

'Are you sure he wasn't offended?' said Francesca.

'He has a hide like a rhinoceros,' replied Giles.

'That is a new expression for me. I like it,' she said.

'So, the other reason for the visit. We know Donaldson is already thinking about a further level. We need to hurry him up,' said Giles, but more to the point, we need workbooks very soon to broaden the sales.'

'You should have met Signor Martini,' said Francesca, 'The director of NIE. He has said the same thing. Even more, Marco, who is the area manager in Bari has said this. From our point of view, *superiore* and universities are the target market. Private language schools are good, but they have small classes. When we sell to a private language schools, students keep the books. We sell more to the next class. This is not so in state schools. Unlike England, parents must pay for school books. They will keep the book and pass it from brother to sister to cousin to neighbour. There is a rule in some schools that texts must be adopted then kept for at least five years to allow this. In the universities and colleges, there is a busy … thriving?'

Giles nodded.

'Thriving second-hand market. A workbook must be designed so that students write in answers to the exercises for homework. Then they can be used only once and we sell new ones every year.'

'We are singing from the same hymn sheet,' said Giles.

'Another new expression, thank you. Surely he understands this argument?'

'Our problem is that he will insist on doing them himself. This is the kind of thing editors could do in-house very quickly.'

'At NIE … in Italy generally … we believe in the importance of the author,' she said, 'It's better that he does them. Quality is important as well as speed.'

Giles felt he had just been told off. 'I agree entirely,' he lied, 'The thing is, we must have them for the Spring sales season. It's early

November. It takes us nine months to a year to produce a book, and that's after we have a finished and edited manuscript.'

'Newspapers produce colour magazines on a weekly schedule,' she said.

Giles knew that Patrick O'Toole, the unpleasant Irish fellow in charge of British sales, had said exactly the same. 'I know that. We have arranged to hurry everything through. I can edit page by page rather than waiting for a finished book. The thing is, he'll need to become a full-time author to do that, then to go on straight away to produce the next level. He's not a bold fellow. Will he be prepared to make the jump?'

'Therefore your task is to push him out of the plane?'

'It is.'

'And my task?'

'Your task is to persuade him that it will sell enough to make a parachute.'

The taxi dropped them at the hotel at ten to midnight. Giles looked up. It had to be ten floors high. It looked new. Concrete and glass. Graham was in a deeply surly mood, continuing to mutter about his workload. They walked through the door into a massive lobby with tall plants, trees almost, shining metal pillars and a gleaming marble floor. It was at least three floors high. It was deserted. Giles glanced sideways to what must be the bar, then to the other side to the restaurant. Both were totally in darkness. Francesca walked the hundred metres to the reception desk and pushed the bell. The night porter emerged grumpily from a back room and Francesca came back with the keys.

'Room 210 ... 211 ... and 212. I asked about room service, but he's the only one on duty and he may not leave the desk. There is no chance.'

Graham harumphed loudly.

'The good thing is we have two nights here. If you put your laundry in by 9 o'clock in the morning, it should be ready by seven p.m.,' she said, 'Certainly, because I'm sure there are very few people here. I could see the boxes for keys, and they were nearly all full.'

Giles stared up at the chandeliers way above them in the lobby, 'Why is it so quiet? Is it the time of year?'

'No, I don't think this is so,' said Francesca, 'The government is investing a lot in the South to bring employment. There are two other new hotels nearby. There is no one to stay in them either ... the employment is in building them,' she lowered her voice, 'Mafia built, I assume. Anyway, Signor Gatti ... Marco ... is meeting us at nine, so it would be wise to have breakfast at eight. As I have explained, Marco is a "law unto himself,"' she smiled in self-satisfaction at getting that expression in, 'So we still do not have a schedule. All I can tell you is that it will be interesting. It always is with Marco.'

Graham brightened up as he looked round the lobby, 'The hotel looks sufficiently international. I assume they will have a proper cooked breakfast. A buffet at least.'

Francesca broke the news, 'Continental only, I'm afraid.'

'How do you do, Signor Gatti,' said Giles.

'No Signor Gatti. Marco! Marco! *Inglese? Non capisco*,' Marco shook hands vigorously with Giles, then kissed Francesca on both cheeks, and patted her bottom repeatedly at the same time. Marco was ursine: huge, dark, hairy and plump. He was in his fifties. He turned to Graham.

'Grey Ham? Dottore Grey Ham!' to Graham's horror he found himself hugged. Marco let fly a stream of voluble Italian, turned back to Graham, and patted him on the shoulder.

'Marco says welcome to Bari,' Marco had understood that and nodded with a huge smile, 'Then he says you must be starving after the food in Milan. He says he is certain it was all lumps of meat in heavy cream sauces, because the Milanese are not Italians at all, but Austrians.'

'Tedesco,' confirmed Marco.

'Or actually Germans,' said Francesca.

'I had something like Wiener schnitzel for lunch,' ventured Graham.

'Si! Wiener schnitzel, *Milanese! Austriaco. Tedesco*,' confirmed Marco, and mimed spitting on the ground. He patted Graham's shoulder more vigorously, '*Andiamo!*'

They walked to the indicated large Opel Rekord Estate car, with Marco talking animatedly to Francesca, who was laughing.

'Rum chap,' whispered Giles to Graham, 'Heart of gold, according to Francesca, and their best area sales manager too.'

They got to the car, and Marco indicated the front seat to Francesca. She shook her head, and said, 'No, no, Graham will sit there. It will be more comfortable.' Marco looked crestfallen.

Graham climbed in and reached for the seatbelt. Marco patted the headrest and spoke to Francesca, then roared with laughter. Francesca frowned and translated, 'He says headrests and seatbelts are a sure sign of a pederast. It is not his fault. They come with the car ... which he adds is made in Germany, not in Italy. He thinks this is amusing. I do not. But he will be insulted if you put on your seatbelt.'

'Then let him be insulted,' said Graham firmly, and clicked the seatbelt into its socket, 'Tell him it is the law in England and we feel uncomfortable without it.'

Francesca translated, and returned, 'He assures you he is an excellent driver and you are safe.'

Marco accelerated hard forward, and skidded sideways alarmingly at the roundabout.

'This is his joke,' said Francesca.

• • •

Francesca explained the itinerary to an increasingly irritable Graham, 'We are visiting a school in Bari. You will not need to speak. Then we drive to Brindisi, just one hundred and twenty kilometres, where you will speak before lunch. Marco expects forty, maybe fifty teachers. We will lunch in Brindisi and drive on to Lecce where you will speak this evening, then we will return here.'

They parked outside a school, and Marco hurried them in. They followed him upstairs to a large office. The principal and six teachers were waiting.

'The English department,' said Francesca.

Graham shook hands all around and instantly forgot their names. Then he shook hands with the principal who spoke in Italian.

Francesca said, 'He hopes that the fresh food here in Puglia will help you recover from the rich and unhealthy meat and cream diet of Lombardy.'

'*Grazie*,' said Giles, who ruefully considered that he had not tasted any of Lombardy's allegedly unhealthy food at all.

'Thank you,' murmured Graham.

The principal handed Graham a copy of *Intercourse* and a pen.

'Please sign,' said Francesca, 'Write "Thank you and best wishes Graham Donaldson."' Graham did as he was told.

'*Andiamo!*' said Marco as soon as the pen left Graham's hand. They followed him out and back to the car. Graham looked at his watch. It was only twenty past nine.

'That was a flying visit,' said Giles, 'We were only there ten minutes, if that.'

'Yes. Courtesy only,' said Francesca, 'It is the largest school, and they have already adopted *Intercourse* for next year. All the schools will follow. They are opinion makers.'

'Please congratulate Marco. That's a fantastic adoption,' said Giles.

Marco spoke quickly.

Francesca nodded, 'Marco says it was no problem. The headmaster is his brother-in-law. The head of English is his cousin.

Also to call and say hello shows our respect, so there is no need to give a talk. The headmaster decides. We are on our way to Brindisi. Job done.'

Graham had hoped to doze. But Marco tapped Graham's arm and pointed at the landscape or buildings at irritating intervals, while Winthrop and Garibaldi chattered in the back seat.

To Graham's horror the car suddenly swerved right onto a bumpy side road, and headed fast up a steep hill. Graham blanched as they drove through a narrow castellated town gate and screeched to a halt on the cobblestones in a square surrounded by ancient stone buildings. Marco was already opening his door. He beckoned to Graham. They all got out. Marco walked to a tree, said a few words to an old woman at a table below it, and then spoke to Francesca.

'He was told the oranges are ripe here,' she translated, 'They are the best in Italy.'

Marco plucked an orange from a tree, whipped out a penknife, peeled it at speed and handed it to Graham, '*Arianca. Mangiare!*'

'Marco says you have never eaten an orange like this before,' she said. Marco was already peeling oranges for Francesca and Giles.

Graham was staring at the orange segments in his hand suspiciously.

'Eat it!' hissed Francesca, 'Go on!'

Graham tentatively put a segment in his mouth. The flavour was indeed remarkably strong, though he worried that it might give him stomach acidity.

'Good lord!' said Giles, 'He's absolutely right. It's just as if I've never tasted an orange before.'

The old woman was filling a bag for Marco. He indicated the oranges in a basket to Graham quizzically.

'No, no, I'm having enough trouble with the blessed olive oil,' he snapped, 'Without carting fresh fruit around the country!'

Marco presented an orange each to Francesca and Giles. 'For later,' she explained.

'*Andiamo!*' said Marco again. They were back in the car. On the main road they drove a few kilometres and turned off into the grounds of a large hospital. Marco drove up to the ambulance entrance where he parked on the crisscross yellow lines, and said something to Francesca. Then he got out with the bag of oranges and headed to the entrance.

'Um, we've come here to deliver the oranges to his son,' said Francesca.

They waited a few minutes. Then Marco emerged with a younger man in full green scrubs who was holding the bag of oranges. They came over to the car, and Giles and Francesca got out.

'Graham,' hissed Giles, 'I think you should stand up and get out.'

The nerve of it! A mere editor telling him what to do. Graham reluctantly got out of the car.

The man in green shook hands, 'Good morning. I am Doctor Gatti. Bruno Gatti. My father wanted me to meet you.'

'Delighted to meet you,' said Francesca, 'I hope we are not disturbing you.'

'No, I am between operations,' he said, then explained, 'I am an orthopaedic surgeon. Hips today.'

'I'm very pleased to meet you, Doctor Gatti,' said Giles.

'Bruno. Please,' was the reply, 'I hope you enjoy your visit to Puglia.'

'Good morning,' mumbled Graham after Francesca had prodded his arm.

Marco smiled, said something to his son, and indicated the car again. 'Brindisi!' he said.

Francesca spoke quietly, 'Marco is very proud of his son. He wanted you to meet him, so that you know his family, and to hear how good his son's English is.'

.   .   .

The car lurched back onto the main road and Marco spoke at length to Francesca who nodded.

'This is for Giles' attention, I think rather than Graham. Marco is unhappy with the binding of the book *Intercourse*. He says it is too strong. He has tried in the office and it is very difficult to pull apart.'

'We have used the best quality paperback binding available,' said Giles, 'It's printed and bound in Hong Kong.'

'This is the problem. I explained how a school book passes around the family for five years or more. Marco says if you use weaker glue, and perhaps print in England, they might fall apart after two,' she paused, 'He may in fact be joking, but I am not sure.'

The audience in Brindisi was around thirty strong. All women, formally dressed. Pearls everywhere. They walked straight in and started. The audience was already seated. Francesca had explained that Marco's assistants from Bari had driven down earlier, and set up the book exhibition with the Brindisi representative. The audience had been given coffee, small pastries, biscuits and had examined the books before they arrived.

'The organisation is like clockwork,' she said.

Marco led them to a restaurant a few hundred metres away. Giles realised that a woman from the talk was walking along with them. She had a tight sheath skirt, plunging neckline, high heels and extremely blonde hair. Her perfume wafted along with her. Giles guessed she was in her forties. They reached the restaurant. Marco indicated the smiling woman and spoke to Francesca, who translated.

'This is Allegra. She was at your talk, and she is a mathematics teacher and she does not speak English. She is having lunch with us ...' Marco said a few more sentences. 'I will explain. She is his good friend, and has volunteered to come with us today. Marco says that we will be embarrassed to speak English all the time, as he does not understand it. He says we will be more relaxed if we sit in the back of the car and converse in English, while he speaks Italian with Allegra in the front.'

Graham felt his eyes widening in shock, 'So three of us will be squashed into the back seat,' he said.

'It is a large car,' said Giles, 'And I'll happily sit in the middle.'

Marco was walking ahead of them to talk to the head waiter.

Francesca whispered, 'For me it is relief. He keeps touching and even pinching my buttocks.' She saw Giles clench his fists.

'No, Giles, it is not serious. He intends it as a compliment. He likes women to feel curted.'

'Curted?' said Giles.

'Yes, he thinks it's a courtesy. To curt women. He will not do this with Allegra here. That's good. Come, we must follow him.'

Giles remembered how Francesca had asked him to correct any errors in her English whatsoever. There hadn't been any of note. Curt? She had obviously extrapolated 'curt' from 'courtesy.' Should he correct her?

She hadn't finished, 'This happens in the South. They like to curt. They are curters. Always curting.'

Giles was on a knife-edge. At this point, having let it go, dare you correct to 'court'?

Graham was perplexed, 'What does "good friend" mean?'

Francesca demurred, 'It is difficult to translate. He actually said *amante*. Er, *amico* is friend, *ragazza* might be girlfriend. Perhaps I may translate *amante* best as "mistress."?'

Graham was appalled, 'Mistress! Does the fellow have no shame? UUP are buying lunch for his mistress? What would this James person say? Haven't you said anything to him?'

Francesca smiled, 'Graham, I really think ... may I be colloquial? That Marco doesn't give a damn what James thinks. Or what I think. Or what you think.'

'Frankly, my dear, I don't give a damn,' said Giles, then seeing Francesca's quizzical frown, 'Clark Gable. *Gone With The Wind*.'

Graham wondered if he were mad.

'There's no menu,' complained Graham.

'No, they have explained the dish of the day, and there is a wide selection of antipasti on the table over there. You can take as much as you want. Bring your plate,' said Francesca, 'Marco has already ordered.'

'How does he know what I want?' said Graham, perusing the three metres long spread of dishes. He didn't know what half of it even was. There were prawns, squid, marinated octopus, mussels, swordfish in thin slices, red peppers, stuffed tomatoes, green and black olives, cucumber, pickled mushrooms, broccoli, rocket, beans of different colours, artichokes, eggplant with parmesan cheese, ricotta.

Francesca grinned, 'Frankly, my dear Graham. He doesn't give a damn.' She saw the look of fury, 'It is a fish restaurant. Marco has ordered tuna.'

'I don't like tinned fish,' said Graham.

'Oh, this won't be tinned.'

Giles was still struggling through the mountain of antipasti he had piled high on his plate when the main course arrived. He had been starving. The tuna was cut in a circle, flat, very thin and filled the entire plate. A bowl of lemon pieces, and another of fresh anchovies were put on the table together with a large bowl of boiled potatoes.

'Wonderful,' Giles managed to say after the first piece, 'I never realised that fresh tuna was, well, like this. I've never seen it. It's more like meat than fish. What do you think Graham? Have you ever had it before.'

'No, I haven't,' said Graham, 'It is quite pleasant.'.

Marco poured them each another glass of wine and called for a third bottle. They had shared a bottle of white with the starter, then Marco had explained that a light red was best for tuna.

Graham was feeling light-headed, slightly sozzled even. 'Are there no drink driving laws here?' He asked.

'Marco knows how much he can drink,' said Francesca.

'Rather a lot apparently,' said Graham.

Marco had spent the meal in animated conversation with Allegra. He declined the offered glass of *mirtilli* blueberry liquor (Giles downed his in one) and led them back to the car. Graham watched him warily. He had to admit he seemed perfectly steady on his feet. Being arm in arm with Allegra helped.

'You will speak at the university in Lecce at five,' said Francesca, 'However, Marco wants you to go to the local NIE office first. Although he lives in Bari, this is his head office. Everything will be ready at the university for the talk in advance, and you should meet everyone and greet them and thank them. This is the regional warehouse, and he will expect you to meet the sales representatives, the people who pack and dispatch the books, the secretaries. Everyone. Even the lady who makes coffee.'

'What? I was not expected to do this in Florence or Milan,' protested Graham.

'This is not Milan,' she said, 'Here people are motivated because they have met you.' Francesca considered that in Graham's case, not having met him was probably more motivating. 'Interestingly, because of its baroque architecture from the time of Charles V, the Holy Roman Emperor, Lecce is known as the Florence of the South,' she paused, 'Though for me, this is a vain boast.'

Dark green metal shelves with books lined every wall. He was shown the warehouse with books stacked everywhere. NIE covered the entire school and university curriculum as well as fiction and non-fiction. The warehouse manager proudly indicated the wide shelves with boxes of *Intercourse* piled high. The green metal desks in the office were crowded together. Graham as instructed, shook hands and said *Grazie* to all and sundry, many of them replied in English, but the lady with a bucket and mop who emerged from the toilet seemed a step too far for him.

During all of this an elderly man with a soft snowy beard wandered in holding a bunch of flowers. He was greeted warmly, and everyone lined up to smell the flowers and comment on the colours.

'This is Antonio, the father of one of the secretaries. He has come in to the office especially to show them some special dahlias from his garden.'

Marco was shaking hands with him, indicating the flowers and praising them extravagantly.

'They all stop work simply to admire an old man's flowers?' queried Graham.

'Oh, yes,' said Francesca, 'They know how to live here. After all, you must agree they are exceptional flowers. Truly beautiful.'

It was a university lecture room. The audience were chatting quietly. Marco led him to the podium. Graham started arranging his notes. He'd got them completely out of order after being hurried out of the previous talk for lunch. These Italians only seemed interested in filling their stomachs. What with annoying teachers asking him questions at the same time he'd been quite discombobulated.

Marco spoke quietly to Francesca.

'He and Allegra don't speak English so they will go now and return at six-thirty,' she explained.

Marco spoke again.

'Ah. Or seven o'clock. There is a small reception in your honour after your talk. Invitation only. They have been told you are a famous author ... a celebrity, and so the university have arranged this. Not NIE,' she added.

'Don't we have to return to our hotel in wherever it is?' he grumbled.

'We will eat in Lecce afterwards,' she said, 'This will be quite a short time. Less than an hour.'

Giles was hovering, 'Er, do you have everything you need for the talk?'

'Yes,' snapped Graham. What a foolish question. 'Where do you think that fellow and his mistress are off to?'

Giles shrugged, 'I have absolutely no idea. I hadn't thought about it.'

'It's hardly behaviour I expected of a UUP representative.'

Francesca interrupted, 'He is employed by NIE. May I say that it's really none of our business?'

'But he has a son. A married man! Bringing his mistress on a business trip!' spluttered Graham, 'Then racing off for doubtless nefarious purposes!'

'Marco is a widower.'

'Oh.'

'Shall I introduce your talk now?'

Giles and Francesca took seats at the back of the hall. Giles noted the talk was almost word for word what Graham had said at Brindisi earlier. He wondered if he should have to attend every talk on the tour. After the large lunch he was also definitely drowsy. Graham's voice was not helping.

Francesca thought the points on the growth of English being aided because it lacked the complexities of gender and inflection was good. It was also so much simpler to have just one second person, 'you' even if his diversion into the history of thee, thou, thy, thyself and thine was perhaps excessive. She was also irritated that his examples were all from French, and that he had skipped the patronizing aspect of using the *tu* form. Did he even know? She could easily transfer the examples to Italian and write them down for him, but then there were the worries about his pronunciation, as well as the fact that the use of Italian by the speaker inevitably led to teachers then asking questions in their mother tongue. As for the forthcoming reception, she had found that one piece of information at a time worked best for Graham's temper.

The reception was in a large wood-panelled room along the hall. It was an entirely different group- none of the English teachers from his talk were there. The group were immaculately dressed, the men and women looked formal and dignified, and uniformed waiters hovered with trays of glasses. Everyone was chatting in Italian. As they walked in a waiter said, 'Champagne?'

They each took a glass. 'Don't be disappointed,' Francesca whispered to Giles, 'It will really be Prosecco. We use the word champagne quite loosely.'

Graham was thirsty after his talk. He downed his glass in one. The waiter immediately handed him another. He hiccupped. 'It's extremely fizzy,' he said.

'A characteristic of sparkling wine,' murmured Francesca. She felt sarcasm was beginning to suit her.

Graham hiccupped again.

'Hold your breath,' suggested Giles. What were the other cures? Shock? He could hardly shout suddenly in the crowded room in such dignified company. Ice cube down the back? Graham might not take kindly, 'Or take a long drink ...'

Graham swallowed all of the second glass of Prosecco and burped sickeningly.

'I actually meant water ...' said Giles.

Graham hiccupped again. An interesting thought struck him. It was often spelled 'hiccoughed' but pronounced 'hiccupped.'

'Should I pat your back?' asked Giles solicitously.

'Certainly ...hiccup ... not!' Graham held his breath until he felt light-headed. A suppressed hiccup? Was that the last one? He remembered stories of people who had hiccupped for days, months, years, for decades even, a lifetime, with no cure ever being found. A wave of panic and self-pity descended. Was he to be stuck here with all these foreigners, while hiccupping uncontrollably for the rest of his days? Why on Earth had he had that disgusting wine forced on him?

Francesca circulated and spoke to a few people, then waited till Graham had calmed, 'The thing is, they'd like you to say a few words ... about the value of English.'

'What?'

'The other thing is, few if any of them speak English. The idea is that you speak, and I translate - a couple of minutes at a time.'

'What am I supposed to say?'

'Platitudes? It doesn't matter much. It's just a social occasion. Your presence is an excuse. I spoke to one gentlemen and asked what he taught at the university. He didn't. He was invited by his cousin because he had a nice suit and with his white hair, a most distinguished appearance. He's an undertaker. His cousin's in charge of accounts. It's all about goodwill. It's important here, and we're hoping the university will adopt.'

'I thought you were aiming at secondary modern,' said Graham.

'*Scoula media* isn't exactly...' she changed tack, 'It's also ideal for the scientists and engineers who have to complete a first year English credit. They'll have done English in *superiore* but will remember little of it.'

Graham waited while Francesca introduced him to a burst of applause. He coughed, 'The history of the English language reveals that it embraces elements of Anglo-Saxon, Old Norse, French and Church Latin, as well as words from languages as diverse as American Indian, Spanish, Portuguese, German, Dutch. Some date from the British Empire. For example, Hindi ... bungalow, veranda, jungle, tiffin ..., Malay, caddy and gingham, and Chinese, ketchup of course, and cha, which is an informal word for tea, as in a cup of cha,... hiccup,' Damn. The hiccups had not completely gone.

Francesca took over at once and spoke animatedly for several minutes, then gestured to him.

Graham got back to his feet, 'The social history of Saxons and Normans after 1066 is displayed in the Germanic origin of words for animals, which the lowly Saxon peasants tended in the fields in contrast to the French origin of our words for meat. Or meats. It's untrue that meat is necessarily uncountable. Compare loaves and fishes. The Norman nobles never touched the animals in the fields, but only saw them cooked on a platter with a sprig of herbs,' he paused for laughter which did not come, 'For example we have beef, mutton and pork from French 'bouef,' 'mouton' and 'porc', and sheep and pig, and indeed sow, from the German 'schafe' and 'schwein' and 'sau'...'

Francesca was already speaking over him, which continued. He sat down. To his surprise she got several bursts of laughter and also clapping. This continued, with Graham speaking for a minute to utter silence then Francesca speaking for three minutes to laughter and applause. When she finished she indicated Graham and there was a resounding ovation. Graham blushed and bowed slightly. A waiter handed him a glass of Prosecco. Graham raised it. There was more applause.

Giles caught up with her, 'What on Earth were you saying? Your translation was immensely popular.'

'Oh, I didn't translate. It was too esoteric, even boring, for them. I did a completely different talk about English eccentricity ... driving on the wrong side, warm beer, chips with everything, garden gnomes and so on. They particularly enjoyed the section on public schools and fagging and beating. So thank you for telling me that. Don't tell Graham!'

Marco turned up at a quarter past seven with Allegra. Francesca noted that he had changed from a white shirt to a crisp blue one, and Allegra's hair was still damp. She was aware that Marco had his own office in the NIE building at Lecce with a private bathroom, and that everyone would have gone home. Would Graham notice?

The simple meal in Lecce consisted of a trio of pastas, washed down with *Primitivo di Manduria* red wine. There was orecchiette with broccoli and anchovies; cavatelli pasta with rocket, tomatoes, garlic and olive oil; more pasta with oyster mushrooms and sausage. There was crusty white bread and small bowls of pungent green olive oil.

'Marco says this is the very best olive oil in all of Puglia, which means in all of Italy. So please don't mention our bottles of Tuscan oil,' Francesca added, 'Which is far superior in fact.'

Graham remembered he still had to lug that bottle around for the rest of his travels, if not the remainder of his days.

Giles, whose voice was rather slurred, asked Francesca how he could make his UUP editorial department contribution to the meal.

In fact he was so pleasantly mellow he suggested that editorial could pay for the entire meal.

'Anywhere else, yes,' said Francesca, 'And thank you. But not here. Marco would be insulted. This is all paid for by NIE.'

Graham wondered again about Marco's driving ability after the quantities of alcohol, especially as they set off at some considerable speed. They drove into Brindisi to drop off Allegra ... Marco gallantly went into the building and saw her upstairs to her apartment door while they waited for what must have been well over fifteen minutes. Giles was snoring very gently, his chin on his chest.

Francesca said, 'I hope he's not too long. We have an early train to catch to Naples tomorrow.'

'How early?' said Graham suspiciously.

'The eight-ten train. It is between four and five hours on the train, but we should arrive in time for some lunch. You have your talk at four thirty. Then a question and answer session. This will be the largest audience so far.'

Eventually, Marco returned, the car started again and Marco spoke to Francesca.

'He says we will stop in the popular seaside town of Monopoli for dessert on the way to Bari. He says this café has the best ice-cream in the whole of Italy and that you must try especially the pistachio. Also there are numerous varieties with fresh fruit. The cherry is famous and you should try also the bergamot.'

'I am actually rather tired,' said Graham.

'It is a small detour. He says you will be delighted with the ice cream. You will need four or five types. Marco had wanted to bring Allegra, as she loves ice cream, but that would have meant driving back to Brindisi afterwards, and Marco expects you'll want to be in bed very early, even by twelve.

'Marco knows what's right from wrong. Tell the people, Marco, tell them you're a liar. Tell them what a liar you are. Come on liar, you know what you done.'

'Animal! You go down on your knees to me!'

They had spent some time rehearsing the knife fight. It was one of Malcolm O'Reilly's greatest death scenes, and there had been a few. He turned to the audience, arms outstretched, and bit into the blood capsule. He tasted the sherbet, always a pleasant sensation, and let the foaming red trickle down his chin before collapsing flat out on the stage.

The lights went down on the stage, and the spotlight hit Barry Grant, now allowed to play the closing role of the narrator, the lawyer Mr Alfieri, in spite of his feeble efforts at an American accent. In recompense, he had managed to improve Marco and Rodolpho's Italian accents. Malcolm O'Reilly had been deaf to Barry's suggestion that he play the role of one of the two Italian immigrants to Brooklyn.

'No, no, dear boy. Marco has to be tall, rough and sturdy.

Rodolpho has to be, well, rather an effete and pretty boy, and unfortunately you do not fulfil either criterion.'

Arthur Miller's *A View From The Bridge* was one of the favoured plays which were enacted in a rehearsed and costumed reading (with movement and action) once a month on a Wednesday evening at World English Centre. Most of the cast read, but Malcolm and Gloria shone because they knew their lines and so were not hampered by holding a book. In Malcolm O'Reilly's eyes, the play counted as extremely modern, dating back a mere twenty years or so to when Anthony Quayle had performed the part of Eddie Carbone, Malcolm O'Reilly's role tonight. He had seen the 1956 production in London. The play had seemed apposite just before his trip to Italy.

The story was set in Red Hook, Brooklyn. Eddie, an American citizen and longshoreman, takes in two relatives, illegal immigrants from Italy, Marco and his younger brother Rodolpho. They have been smuggled in by the Mafia, who find them jobs. They will have to repay their travel one day. Marco works hard to send money back to his family. Rodolpho spends his wages on clothes and records. Eddie grows jealous of his niece Catherine's interest in Rodolpho, whom he considers effeminate. Eddie cannot admit to himself that he fancies Catherine, though his wife Beatrice suspects. In the end, Eddie shops Marco and Rodolpho to the immigration authorities so that they will be deported. Marco takes his revenge with a knife.

The lights went up, Malcolm stumbled to his feet, somewhat awkwardly, another theatrical triumph. The students applauded furiously. He tried hard to hold his stomach in. Perhaps, Gloria (who was playing Beatrice) had been right in suggesting that a string vest and jeans were unsuitable attire at his age.

He put out his arms to beckon Marco, Rodolpho and Catherine to the front. That's the magnanimous gesture of the star of the show.

Barry as Mr Alfieri remained on his side platform (a table with a cloth over it, and a chair on top) uncertain whether to climb down and join them.

Phil was playing Marco for the fourth time in two years, and stepped forward cheerfully, waving his rubber knife over his head.

The recent addition to the teaching staff, Damian, had played Rodolpho for the first time tonight. As ever, Malcolm had rehearsed a light peck for the scene where Eddie kisses Rodolpho on the mouth to indicate that Rodolpho is effeminate. On the actual performance, he had given him a full slobbering kiss to elicit the shock that added so much impact to the performance. It was his standard trick. No one had ever played Rodolpho a second time.

Jeanette had also just played the niece, Catherine, for the first time. She had been taken in by Malcolm's other trick, where he seized Beatrice's dressmaking shears and held them to Catherine's throat. It had not been rehearsed, and Jeanette had been terrified. She touched her neck again and looked at her hand for signs of blood. She was sure he must have actually cut her.

Both Damien and Jeanette stayed as far away from Malcolm O'Reilly as they could as they took their bows. Damien was desperate to get off and wash his mouth and Jeanette was equally desperate to check her neck in a mirror. The two immigration officers skulked at the back unnoticed.

A Swiss-German girl, Heidi, walked up the aisle in the centre and presented Gloria with a massive bouquet of flowers, an event which was repeated in every production, and which would decorate their house for a week afterwards. True, Beatrice was hardly the leading role, but Malcolm felt justified in ordering the flowers at WEC's expense. Gloria was not a teacher after all, so had no benefit from the kudos of performing.

'Drinks in the Green Room,' proclaimed Malcolm as they walked off. The Green Room was in fact just a classroom, Room 14, adjoining the stage, which was at one end of the school's large restaurant. 'It's Prosecco tonight. As you know, Gloria and I are departing for Rome on Friday. I decided to dispense with the Pomagne his month and get in the Italian mood with Prosecco.'

Gloria cornered Jeanette when she got back from checking her neck in the ladies. 'I hope Malkie didn't scare you, dear. It's his little trick. He does it every time. You have to laugh. Your face! You should've seen it.'

'I was absolutely fucking terrified,. I thought he'd totally lost it,' said Jeanette, then wondered if the F-word was appropriate to the boss's wife.

'That's nothing, dear. You want to try doing *Private Lives*. It's another one we do regularly. You know it, dear? The couples both have fights? Malkie's a heavy man to have lying on top of you, especially the time he tripped and fell right onto me. Mind, the weight of a man can be enjoyable sometimes. He used to get over-excited during the action if you take my meaning. When he was younger, that is. Quite a bit younger. I could feel it against my leg, well, thigh. I had bruises all over after the Scarborough run.'

'I haven't seen the play,' said Jeanette, wondering how she could get away, 'Nor read it.'

'Everyone knows *Private Lives!* It's Noël Coward.'

'Not me.'

'Have you been teaching here long, dear?' asked Gloria.

'Just a few weeks. I was teaching in Italy last year, at a private school in Turin.'

'Ooh! We're off to Italy on Friday. Is Turin near Rome?'

'No,' said Jeanette, 'It's in the north.'

'Is it true what they say about Italian men?'

'I don't know,' said Jeanette, 'What do they say?'

'Randy buggers. Hands all over the place. Bum pinchers.'

'It used to be, I heard. Nowadays younger women would make a fuss.'

Gloria considered, 'Malkie gets very protective. He won't stand for that sort of vulgar behaviour.'

'I'm sure you'll be absolutely fine, um, my boyfriend's Italian.'

'Well, I'm sure he's not like that then,' said Gloria, 'I mean, not like all the rest of them.'

Malcolm O'Reilly glanced over at Gloria. He hoped she was not referring to him as 'Malkie' to his staff members. Not that he'd ever managed to stop her in the past. 'Another drink, Damian? I so hope you weren't too startled. Dear Larry Olivier always believed that you can't fake that sort of thing. It's such a dramatic moment.'

Damian could still taste the soap, in spite of the second glass of Prosecco.

'I wonder if you'd be interested in performing in *Private Lives* next month? I feel you and Jeanette would be ideal for Victor and Sybil, the younger pair.'

Damian coughed, best to laugh it off, 'I don't suppose you'll be kissing me in that one.'

'Of course not. Though Gloria will, obviously.'

Malcolm O'Reilly looked round peevishly at Barry Grant. Barry had the habit of hovering. Hovering without participating. The man must want something, 'Barry. Thank you so much for ...' no adjective was coming to mind. An adequate? A reasonable? An under-stated? An inaudible? No, he would have to lie, '... an excellent performance as Mr Alfieri.'

'Thank you, Malcolm. I was worried about the American accent. I don't think I quite got it right. Um, I could do him as Italian next time.'

'No, no, Barry. The point is that the lawyer Alfieri, Eddie Carbone and Beatrice are either American born or have been there since early childhood. Catherine was born there certainly. They need to contrast with Marco and Rodolpho who are new arrivals.'

'Yes, that puzzled me,' said Barry, 'They've just arrived. They have strong accents, but actually decent grammar.'

'The play is by Arthur Miller!' said Malcolm, 'Beyond criticism. Your accent was, well, no doubt it would have sounded reasonably American to our audience of non-English speakers.'

'Thank you,' said Barry doubtfully, 'Um, I wanted to ask you a favour.'

'Go on.'

'Could you take a couple of books to Rome for Gabriella? They're for her Applied Linguistics course. I found second-hand copies. They're in the staff room.'

Malcolm O'Reilly was aware that he could hardly decline. He already had two cardboard boxes of WEC brochures for the conference, and it was inconceivable that Gloria would be travelling light. Then second-hand books? He had no desire to put dusty volumes speckled with brown foxing spots and full of book mites next to his clean shirts. 'How heavy are they?' he asked. Then realized he had said it rather brusquely.

Barry noted the furrowed brow, 'You know that you can carry reading matter on the flight by hand. It's not part of your allowance. They're a bit heavy to post.'

'Mills and Boone romances are rather more to Gloria's reading taste for a plane journey,' Malcolm said. Good, that should sound jocular, 'Yes, yes. Of course, dear boy. As long as it's not the complete twelve volumes of the Oxford English Dictionary. Go and fetch them for me.'

They had a compartment to themselves. Giles put his case and Francesca's case on the luggage rack. Graham coughed, and when Giles turned around, handed him his case and carrier bag too.

'Do ensure the olive oil remains upright,' he said, 'Perhaps I might have the window seat?'

Giles had been about to sit there, opposite Francesca. 'Of course,' he replied, 'Would you prefer to travel with your back to the engine or facing the direction of travel? I'm sure Francesca won't mind moving.'

'Yes, perhaps with my back to the engine? I believe it's safer in case of a train crash.'

Francesca stood, and he took her seat. 'Do you mind if I sit opposite, or would you prefer the extra leg room?' she said. Sarcasm was beginning to be fun.

'Sit where you wish,' Graham said. Francesca took the window seat and Giles settled next to her.

'You would have thought they'd have had an English newspaper at the station kiosk,' Graham said.

'Not in Bari,' she replied, 'Perhaps in Rome or Milan. They might have *The Times* or the international edition of *The Daily Mail*.'

'I was hoping for *The Daily Telegraph*,' complained Graham.

'That's unlikely, I'm afraid,' Francesca said, 'Don't you have a book?'

'I shall make some notes,' Graham said. 'Though I had planned on doing the *Telegraph* crossword.'

Giles saw the chance, 'Ah, notes for an accompanying Workbook, or the next level of *Intercourse?*'

'I was thinking of the ensuing level. I wonder whether a Workbook is absolutely necessary'

'Essential,' said Francesca, 'In Italian schools homework must be set, and teachers will prefer to have a linked Workbook.'

'We are getting exactly the same feedback from Greece, Spain and France,' added Giles.

'It's most important for the sales representatives,' said Francesca, 'It will increase sales of the series exponentially.'

'The Workbooks are a most profitable element,' said Giles, 'Little or no illustration. Easy to prepare. They don't need the highest paper quality either. Then as we will design them for students to write in, they will not be passed on second-hand."

'I had thought that UUP was a non-commercial publisher,' said Graham.

'Everyone has to eat,' said Giles, 'Editors, designers, illustrators, typesetters, printers, paper manufacturers, transport drivers ...'

'And authors. For the author this should mean eating in the finest restaurants,' said Francesca, 'Current sales are already exciting. This will be the ... the ...'

'Cherry on top of the cake?' suggested Giles.

'Thank you, Giles. Another new idiom. Indeed and the jam and cream in the centre plus the icing also.'

'We just say the cherry,' said Graham, who was wondering whether it was worth a note.

'In short, it means a great deal of money,' finished Giles.

'I shall consider it. Now if you'll excuse me, I must make some notes.'

Giles coughed, 'Time is of the essence. We were hoping you might finish the Workbook sooner rather than later.'

'I have a full time teaching position!' said Graham, 'I have no intention of working myself into an early grave.'

'It may be at times such as this that the position of a full-time author would look attractive,' said Francesca carefully.

Graham glared at them. Did they believe that he, Graham Donaldson, was too stupid to perceive a rehearsed double act? So that was what they were after. It was not as if he had never considered it. There were attractions. No more lessons with tedious young adults. No more having to suffer the constant badgering and pestering of his colleagues. No more pontificating from Malcolm O'Reilly.

Money was not a prime motivation in his life nor any motivation at all. He had had lodging and board with Mrs Read in Sebastopol Road for ten years, not that he had ever discovered her first name, though letters were addressed to Mrs E. Read. Possibly it was Elizabeth, or given her age and formality, perhaps 'E' was her late husband's initial. Ernest? Eric? Edward? One of those. Not Ethelbert, surely? He snickered. Ethelbert. Most amusing. Maybe she was an Ethel. Or an Enid. The food was good plain fare, and at least there was no responsibility for cooking, or laundry. More importantly he need not be concerned with mortgages or gas and electricity bills, matters about which his colleagues at WEC were continually complaining. Graham did not own a car, and strolled the few hundred yards to the school daily, rain or shine. Rain or shine? Interesting expression. One to note. Holidays were simply days on which he did not go into the school. Mrs Read, a widow of increasingly advancing years, allowed him full use of the front parlour in the evenings, and there was an oak bureau, purchased by the late husband, upon which he could write. On the other hand, this trip had exposed him to large bedrooms with double beds and en-suite facilities. Showers? He was not an American. Baths were perfectly sufficient. No doubt one could become accustomed to duvets. He had quite liked them. The dining experiences had been novel and illuminating though travelling was unpleasant in the extreme. The bottle of olive oil came to mind. What would Mrs Read make of that? She was the only potential recipient. He had never given her a gift before, though he believed those who took foreign trips were often expected to give small gifts on return. Gifts. You presented gifts. Or presents. Was that the origin of a 'present'? You presented it? He supposed it must be. The mantlepiece in the front parlour was festooned with small ornaments which Mrs Read had received from her more adventurous relatives. Dutch clogs made of blue and white china. A windmill of the same material and hue. A crudely modelled china Eiffel Tower. A small wooden model of a cuckoo clock with 'Interlaken' inscribed upon it. Olive oil, however, would not be a feature of her culinary experience. Graham remembered how his mother would use small bottles of clear olive oil from Boots The Chemist for softening ear wax. He shifted in his seat. The greenish Italian oil had certainly proven efficacious in softening the contents of one's stomach.

Giles had seen Graham drift into a reverie before. It was a feature of editorial meetings. He leaned forward, 'A penny for your thoughts.'

Graham looked up. What an odd expression. His mother used to say it. Spend a penny. A penny for the guy. Not a penny to your name. Ten a penny. The penny has dropped. A penny arcade. In for a penny, in for a pound. Penny wise, pound foolish. Not a 'new penny' for your thoughts. After seven years the word 'new' before penny had virtually disappeared. 'What?'

'You seemed lost in thought.'

'Yes.'

'The advantages of building upon the success of *Intercourse* are obvious to us as publishers,' said Giles.

'I have not received any money from UUP yet,' said Graham, 'Not a penny,' he chuckled, 'Nor a new penny.'

'Indeed not. As you will recall, royalties are paid annually and are paid six months after the accounting date, which is July 31st. So on December 31st, you should receive the initial cheque which will cover the two and a half months after publication in the Spring. However, in the circumstances, we would be prepared to pay you an advance against future earnings immediately, should you be prepared to devote yourself entirely to the project,'

Giles watched Graham's face carefully. He looked confused, 'My suggestion is that you ask World English Centre for a year's sabbatical ... unpaid. In that way you would keep the security of your employment until substantial royalties ... and we believe they will be substantial ... come in. The advance we are proposing would be your current annual salary,' he paused just as James had told him to, 'Plus fifty per cent.'

Graham scowled, 'Should we be discussing my personal financial arrangements in front of a third party?'

'Oh. You mean me,' said Francesca.

'I am sure you can rely on Ms Garibaldi's absolute discretion as a senior representative of the company.'

Graham was doing calculations. He had considerably more than his annual salary resting in his bank account. Years of frugality had allowed him to amass the sum. Would an advance give the publisher power? He could easily survive without it, and having no strings attached would enhance his negotiating position in the face of future editorial interference. He had little fear that WEC would not keep his job open. How could O'Reilly dispense with a soon-to-be famous author? He would be able to use Mrs Read's front parlour as an office. 'I shall require a few days to consider your proposal,' he said.

'Hopefully you can make a decision by Sunday in Rome?' said Giles.

'I don't understand why I have to come too, Malkie!' protested Gloria.

'They need to enter the amount of foreign exchange in both of our passports,' said Malcolm O'Reilly, 'Given Dr Schaffhauser's generous per diem, we should take the maximum amount of lire.'

'Fifty pounds each! Will we need that much?'

'And fifteen pounds each in sterling,' he said, 'We should make the most of it.'

'Everybody puts a couple of ten pound notes in their socks,' she said, 'You remember when we went to the Costa Brava? I got a corn I had so much stuffed in my shoe. I hobbled off that plane.'

He shuddered at the memory of the Spanish holiday, two years previously. Gloria had developed an instant affection for Spanish brandy. The generous bar service on the flight had contributed to the hobbling as well. 'I should imagine that would be the first place they'd look,' said O'Reilly, 'I shall simply place additional funds inside a book.' One of the linguistics books, he thought. They both had the names of the previous owner inscribed in them, and he could claim total surprise if the money were to be found. A short but pleasant conversation with Lorenzo Giordano, a beautifully attired student on the Business English for Executives course had resulted in the exchange of a further forty pounds for lire.

'Lire?' said the bank clerk, 'Are you off somewhere nice, Mr O'Reilly?'

'Rome,' he said, 'It's a business trip,' he added proudly.

'The eternal city of the seven hills,' said the clerk, 'Mrs Dickenson and I spent our honeymoon there. It was advertised as Seven Days on the Seven Hills.'

'How romantic,' said O'Reilly.

Gloria butted in, 'And seven nights. I'm hoping for a second honeymoon myself, if you know what I mean.' She nudged O'Reilly sharply in the ribs, 'We could do with a bit of romance.'

'I had my pocket picked in the Colosseum,' said the clerk glumly,

'Fortunately, what with such strict exchange controls there was very little in the wallet. Just a ten shilling note.'

'How unfortunate,' said O'Reilly.

'The wallet had great sentimental value. It was my father's,' said the clerk, 'He gave it to me just before he passed away.'

'Oh, dear, how very sad,' said O'Reilly.

'It was. There was a picture of my late mother that he'd carried for years. The only copy.'

'I'm sorry.'

'Do be careful of the shellfish,' said the clerk, 'Mrs Dickenson was most unwell. It lasted the whole time we were in Rome.'

'Still, mainly happy memories, I'm sure,' said O'Reilly brightly.

'I don't know,' said the clerk doubtfully, 'It rained nearly every day. The hotel was extremely noisy. I wouldn't ever go back there myself.'

'Gloomy bugger,' said Gloria as they left the bank.

'He did pour cold water on the trip,' said O'Reilly. He looked at his watch, 'I'm sure they're managing perfectly well without me at the school. Perhaps we should have a coffee, then I'll run you home.'

The Naples hotel was a bright new building on the harbour, right by the boat dock for the trips to Capri. Each floor had a row of large tinted glass windows, reflecting the bay beyond. Behind it the narrow streets curved uphill, with washing hanging to dry on lines strung between the high buildings.

Francesca dealt with reception, 'Fortunately all of our rooms are ready before time. As I have explained, we will be here for one night. There is only one talk today, then tomorrow we have the British Council and Sorrento. We have a couple of hours before the talk too.

We could have a light lunch in the coffee shop. Or would you prefer to rest?'

'I'm rather hungry,' said Giles.

'Excellent,' she said, 'Graham?'

'Yes, yes. Lunch.'

'So we'll meet in fifteen minutes? By the way, in this hotel, it will be perfectly safe to leave your valuables in the room,' she said, 'It would be preferable in fact rather than taking them with you.'

'You told us before not to leave anything valuable in the hotel rooms,' said Graham.

'This hotel is different. No one would ever dare steal from the guests here.' Francesca saw that both men looked puzzled, 'The hotel is a legitimate business,' she looked around and lowered her voice, 'But is, how shall I say, as the Americans will, it is, I believe, connected.'

They were looking blankly at her.

'Camorra operated,' she whispered.

'Camera what?' said Graham loudly.

'Shh ... I said Camorra. It is the mafia of Campania ... this region. The Mafia is Sicily. Then in Calabria it is the 'Ndrangheta. In Sardinia the Anonima Sarda. The Camorra is similar to these but in Napoli. They are said to be the most violent.'

'Good Lord!' said Graham, 'Why are we staying here?'

'Because it is very safe. The safest. Also the cleanest. They will not, er, go to the toilet upon their own back gardens, or do you say door step? No one will steal here. No one will clean the rooms badly. The chefs will wash their hands most carefully. The waiters will be attentive and polite. It is efficient, you see how our rooms were ready? It is how these "men of honour" invest their money. They are in actuality popular in poor regions, because they replace the police.'

Giles nodded, 'To live outside the law you must be honest.'

It was Francesca's turn to join Graham in looking blank.

'Sorry,' said Giles, 'Bob Dylan. *Absolutely Sweet Marie.* To live outside the law you must be honest.'

'You were saying on the train that your great love is the classical music,' said Francesca, 'You mentioned Stravinsky and Bartók.'

'Yes. And Bob Dylan. It's a song on *Blonde on Blonde*.'

'The world's gone mad,' muttered Graham.

Graham closed the door behind the porter. At last a fellow who had not hovered for a gratuity. The room was the largest of the trip so far. He walked over to the floor to ceiling darkened glass window. See Naples and die. Wasn't that the expression? Sightseeing had never been an interest, but he had to admit that the view across the deep blue bay would be counted spectacular if you liked that sort of picture postcard thing, even if the wall of glass made him feel giddy. He looked around the room. A television. An extravagance. It would all be in Italian, not that he would wish to watch it even if it were in English. A large double bed. Light switches all over the place. A large gilt-framed painting of Roman buildings in ruins. Pompeii presumably, judging by the dramatically smoking volcano in the background. Would Naples be vulnerable to a new eruption? That was something to lie awake worrying about in the early hours. No doubt the locals banished it from their minds. The bathroom was black marble tiles with gold taps. Graham tutted at the sheer vulgarity. Bath robe. Thick soft towels. A row of small bottles of perfumed unguents and lotions that he would have no use whatsoever for. He picked one up by its gold top: conditioner, whatever that might be. Another was body lotion. Hand cream. After-shave. Shampoo at least was familiar. This was the sort of room that beckoned to a future professional author, even one who hitherto had eschewed luxuries. And there, just as the porter had placed it, was that British Airways bag with the olive oil.

The talk was downstairs in the hotel conference centre, which was new. The room capacity was 212, and every gilded metal seat was soon to be full, with more people standing at the back and sides.

Giles stood with Graham at the lectern, gazing at the crowd. Francesca was out front, showing people to their seats, shaking hands, kissing cheeks.

A man came over and shook hands, 'I am Dario Esposito, the representative for this area. I must apologize that I cannot entertain you to dinner this evening. My daughters have a music recital at school, and of course I must attend. Francesca knows the city well. You are in good hands. I will escort you tomorrow ... I look forward to it.'

Giles thanked him, and asked which instruments his daughters played. Graham just stood there as Giles prattled on. He had no idea why the difference between a violin and a viola, whatever it might be, was worth so much verbiage.

'Have you noticed Italian audiences,' said Giles pensively, 'Italians in general. They're most physically attractive people. Well-dressed. Well-groomed. Good looking. The men as well as the women. Beautiful women. Handsome chaps too, most of them.'

Graham followed Giles' gaze. He had been staring straight at Francesca Garibaldi, 'I hadn't noticed, Winthrop. I suppose you mean in a Latin sort of way.'

'Naturally in a Latin way,' said Giles, 'Virtually by definition.'

The conversation took Graham back to World English Centre, with the predatory male teachers staring out of the staff room window, and remarking crudely on the physical attributes of the women students passing below. Thank goodness the influx of female teachers had ameliorated that sort of behaviour. Dampened it down. Put a lid on it. At least Winthrop was remaining on the side of polite comment.

'Awfully good-looking people,' added Giles, 'Likeable too. Jolly good food. Excellent wine. What did you think about the view of the Bay of Naples from the rooms? Quite mesmerising. I rather thought I'd drawn the short straw in being assigned Italy, rather than France or Greece, but now, you know, I really welcome it.'

'I see,' said Graham, 'Now if you'll excuse me, Winthrop, I should put my notes in order.'

They assembled in the lobby at seven-thirty that evening. Francesca was carrying the green Alitalia bag with her olive oil.

'We have a short errand to deliver the oil to Giovanni's friend. I think we should consider his friend's restaurant for dinner, but we may prefer my favourite, which has a view of the bay. We should walk. It is only a few hundred metres.'

Graham wondered if he could offer his olive oil too. Perhaps not.

The street was narrow and so noisy. In the daytime the tall apartment buildings blocked out most of the light, with the festooned washing on lines across the street blocking out the rest.

'It must be near here,' said Francesca, 'Number thirty-two, but I see no restaurant sign.' She stopped at a heavy oak door with black metal handles, 'Can this be it?' She hammered with the door knocker.

The door opened a crack, a man's face appeared. Francesco spoke in Italian. They heard Giovanni, and Firenze and *olio d'oliva*.

'*Prego* ...' the door opened. Giles and Graham followed her in. Absolute silence. There was a long table at the end. Perhaps a dozen middle-aged and elderly men were sitting there with tumblers and bottles of wine. In front of them were three smaller tables with two men in black suits and white shirts at each table, staring straight at them. There was no wine on their tables.

Francesca murmured nervously and handed over her bottle of olive oil. The man who had opened the door thanked her profusely, kissed her on both cheeks. He held his hands wide and explained something in rapid Italian. Francesca was nodding furiously, and repeating *Grazie* at high speed.

'Come,' she said and beckoned them to the door which shut loudly behind them. Francesca walked rapidly down the hill for twenty metres or so. The men scurried after her.

Francesca stopped, 'Madonna!' she exclaimed. She drew a deep breath, 'The proprietor, Giovanni's friend and associate, has explained that the restaurant has been reserved tonight for a private business dinner. Otherwise, we would have been his welcome and honoured guests ... he apologises profusely that he cannot entertain us, though he has invited us to come tomorrow if we wish. I don't wish. I think you understand what kind of private business dinner this is and who it is for. The younger men at the small tables will be bodyguards. The older men are ...'

'Mafia!' said Giles.

'Camorra,' she corrected. 'I think so.'

Graham was shaking, 'We could all have been killed! Kidnapped!'

'There was absolutely no danger, I can assure,' Francesca said. 'We walked into a social event. He knows Giovanni. No one would harm us.'

'Criminals!' said Graham.

'I expect,' she said, 'Though their custom is reputed to be a sign of an excellent restaurant. These people value their food. However, he has recommended an alternative restaurant to us. It is in the street on the right. He believes we will like it.'

They turned the corner. Graham looked around, 'It appears to be a most insalubrious area.'

'Inside the apartments will be immaculate. We do not worry so much on the exterior of old buildings. It must be this one.'

They were standing outside a lit window. Menus were posted next to the door. They looked through the window into the dimly lit interior. The floor was rough and uneven stone slabs. The tables looked old with red and white gingham tablecloths. A couple of elderly men were playing cards. Tumblers of red wine were on their table with a half empty carafe and a plate with hunks of bread.

'It looks as if there should be sawdust on the floor,' ventured Giles.

'Oh, dear,' said Graham, 'Oh, dear.'

Francesca was examining the menu, 'The prices are reasonable. I would say too cheap even,' she said. 'I think we should go to my restaurant on the bay.'

She turned. A taxi was cruising slowly down the street. She hailed it. She got in the front seat and Giles and Graham went in the back. She gave directions to the driver and turned, 'I'm sure you will enjoy it. They have a musician with an accordion and a singer.'

The taxi accelerated and drove two hundred metres then stopped. The driver turned, 'English? Yes?'

'My colleagues are English,' said Francesca.

'So? Are you guys fucking crazy? You standing outside the best restaurant in all the Naples. Then you get in my cab, and instruct to a touristic place at ten times price! Why for?'

'I know this restaurant on the bay,' said Francesca.

'I know also. I collect often. Rich dumb Americans from the tourist ships. This is what it is for. You guys not Americans. No?'

Francesca thought quickly, 'I wanted octopus. They do not have on the menu.'

'They have.'

'Not on menu.'

'I will ask.' Suddenly the taxi was reversing terrifyingly fast back up the street. It stopped outside the restaurant. The driver got out, 'Wait. I ask.'

'We should go,' said Graham nervously, 'The driver is quite mad.'

'There will be no octopus. Then he can take us to the other one.'

The driver was coming out. He opened the car door to let Francesca out. 'The cook he has. It is in the fridge for his self dinner. He will cook octopus for you.'

Graham and Giles got out.

'We'll have to go in,' hissed Francesca to them, then to the driver, 'How much do we owe you?'

'Nothing. You don't go nowhere.'

'For your help?'

'I am Neapolitan. I want you to love my city. Go. Eat! Enjoy!' said the driver. He was already climbing back in his car.

'Will I have to eat octopus?' said Graham.

'Only me,' said Francesca, 'But I like it. *Andiamo.*'

They were shown to a table next to the old men, who were now slurping through plates of spaghetti noisily.

'Welcome,' said the owner, 'So you guys not liking my menu? Is OK. Tell me what you want eat. I cook.'

'I'd like to see your menu,' said Giles, 'Or rather perhaps you could recommend for us?'

'OK,' he went to get some menus.

'Do they all have American accents here?' asked Graham.

'Yes.'

'Why?'

'History,' said Francesca, 'The American army was in Naples in large numbers. Then American tourists come to visit Capri and Pompeii. Many Italian-Americans have ancestors from Campania because it was a major emigration area, and they want to see the old country. In the war, the Americans had many personal and family connections in the South who assisted them in the invasion, in Sicily especially, and then here,' she lowered her voice, 'You understand my meaning with "connections" I hope,' she saw

Graham starting to open his mouth, 'But it's better not to say it here.'

'What did you say it was?' said Graham, 'It's very tasty.'

'*Spaghetti al nero di seppie*- with squid ink,' said Francesca, 'Do you like it?'

'It reminds me of Oxo cubes,' said Graham, 'I used to eat them when I was a child.'

Giles looked at him in disbelief.

'It's his pasta of the day, often the best choice,' she said.

For the third time in the meal so far, a shabbily-dressed young boy with a tray came to the table, 'Marlboro?'

Francesca brusquely waved him away.

The boy went to the next table, 'Marlboro?'

'This is a problem,' she said, 'These kids sell in every restaurant here. You see, there is a government tax on cigarettes. You must buy from a kiosk. So when you look at the bay you will see ships in the distance. One today had Marlboro painted all along the side. The ships are outside the customs limit, so small boats go out and buy the cigarettes and sell in the restaurants. Much cheaper.'

'Why don't the police stop them?' said Giles, 'I mean the lad wasn't old enough to buy cigarettes, let alone sell them.'

She shook her head, 'You saw in the other restaurant. There are stronger powers. Marlboro is the very least of their problems.'

Francesca looked at their plates, 'While my octopus is delicious, I wish I could have the same as you. It is unusual in a restaurant on a Thursday evening as it's a popular Sunday lunch here ... *Ragu Napoletano con braciola.*'

'Most unusual,' said Giles.

'Thin pieces of beef escalope with pine kernels and raisins, yes. And of course Parmesan, parsley, basil, tomatoes, white wine ...'

'What a bizarre combination,' said Graham, 'Though most enjoyable.'

'Without the addition of an Oxo cube?' suggested Giles.

Graham furrowed his brow, wondering whether he should take offence. Mrs Read always used Oxo cubes in her cottage pies and beef stews. He had never had complaints about Mrs Read's cooking, but the world of the seasoned traveller ... Graham smirked ... with lots of seasoning on the food ... beckoned.

Francesca said, 'It will be ancient. The pine kernels and raisins are a Greek or an Arab import. I must say, this is a restaurant I shall remember for the future.'

The second rose seller appeared during dessert. There seemed a strict gender divide, pre-teen boys selling Marlboro, pre-teen girls selling flowers.

'*No, grazie*,' said Francesca.

The girl turned to Giles, 'For de lady ...' she wheedled.

'Well, perhaps ...' he started.

'No,' said Francesca firmly, '*Andare via.*' The girl moved to the next table.

'They're so young,' said Giles, 'What are they doing out at this time of night? It can't be safe. Are you sure I mightn't buy you a rose?'

'They are young because they cannot be arrested,' said Francesca, 'And a man will be waiting outside the restaurant for the money. Do not encourage this,' she smiled, 'But you are gallant.'

'Humph,' snorted Graham.

They had paid the bill, tipped generously, and were having coffee along with a complimentary glass of grappa each, which was presented only after the bill had been paid.

'Oh,' said Francesca, 'I was expecting this. This will be the pay-off.'

The taxi driver had come into the restaurant and was shaking hands with the owner, who handed him the grappa bottle and a glass. The driver strolled over to the table, 'Hi. He offers you more grappa,' he said, 'On the house.'

'*Grazie*,' said Francesca, 'Please join us.'

The driver sat down and poured grappa into their glasses as well as his own. 'So, am I right? Is this restaurant better?'

'You are correct, and we thank you,' said Francesca.

They chatted for a few minutes, with the driver enquiring politely the purpose of their visit, and where they lived. Francesca looked at her watch, 'It has been a wonderful meal. Perhaps you could take us back to our hotel?'

The driver laughed, 'I saw you when come out the hotel early this evening. It is five hundred metres. It is a warm night. You do not need a taxi.'

'Well, it is late. We are afraid of walking at night,' she said.

'Fine,' he said, 'I will walk with you. OK? *Andiamo*.'

The driver walked along with them right to the hotel entrance. Francesca tried to put a banknote into his hand, 'Just to thank you for your kindness and good advice,' she said.

The driver waved it away, 'No, *Signora*, this is only friendly. Please. I want nothing. Enjoy your stay. Please come back,' and he strode off back up the hill.

She watched him go, 'Do you know' she said, 'That in the North they say all Neapolitans are bandits and thieves?'

'Neapolitan,' Graham blurted out suddenly. 'Walls made them and Lyons Maid. They came in bars with wafers. Three colours. Strawberry, vanilla and chocolate.'

'You mean ice-cream,' said Giles, wondering yet again about Graham's thought processes.

'It should be strawberry, vanilla and pistachio,' said Francesca, 'The colours of the Italian flag.'

I think one brand was pink, white and green,' said Giles, 'Was it Marks and Spencer? That was when I was a child, though most now use chocolate instead. I suppose English children don't know what pistachio is.'

***

Graham struggled to pull the floor to ceiling curtains closed with great difficulty, not having noticed the cord at one side. The view out at night was disconcerting. Far too much starry sky for his liking.

That olive oil was still there. It was perplexing that it was so valuable that it was worth transporting around the country, then taking the trouble to deliver Francesca's bottle to a restaurant. The scene swam into his mind again. Those cold eyes staring at them. The silence. He shivered. Surely this had been a near-death experience. Why had that irritating woman led him into the proximity of such danger? He would need to have words with James, the managing director, on his return. Especially if he were to enter into so much closer a relationship with UUP. The meals were a considerable compensation.

He started at the sound of a shower next door. That would be Giles. How thoughtless of him. Graham was unused to such frequent ablutions. He went straight to bed, and into a troubled sleep full of Mafiosi, olive oil bottles and colourful ice cream bars.

'Oh, you're both getting in the back then,' grumbled Reg Connor. He was the handyman at WEC, and had been charged with taking Malcolm O'Reilly to Heathrow in the company Ford Granada.

'Mrs O'Reilly is a nervous passenger,' Malcolm replied. 'Thank you Mr Connor. Perhaps you might move the passenger seat forward as far as it will go. I should like the extra legroom.'

'I suppose you want me sitting crushed into the steering wheel too.'

'Not at all. Mrs O'Reilly is of much shorter stature than myself,' he replied, 'She will be sitting behind you,' he looked at his watch, 'When she's ready.'

Gloria was on her second circuit of the house, checking windows, taps, switching off every socket in case electricity leaked out in their absence. O'Reilly had supervised the loading of their bags into the boot, along with the two cardboard boxes of freshly printed brochures.

'Bloody heavy, them boxes,' Reg grumbled, 'They'll knock you for excess baggage for that, Mr O'Reilly.'

'I'm aware of that, Mr Connor.'

O'Reilly reflected. He addressed all teachers by their first names and encouraged them to respond in kind. Yet he always addressed Mrs Tupper formally, and Reg was always Mr Connor, Alf Gillespie, the caretaker, was Mr Gillespie, and Herb, the gardener, was always Mr Wilcox. He was aware that the manual workers would see the use of first names as patronizing. Perhaps he might invite them to use his first name. He looked at Reg Connor who was carefully picking his nose. Perhaps not.

'Gloria!' he called, 'Do hurry up. We were meant to leave ten minutes ago!'

Gloria hurried out, 'Sorry. I needed another tinkle. It'll save stopping on the way. Well, I hope. You know what I'm like when I'm nervous. Hello, Reg. Nice to see you. How's Jean?

'Morning, Mrs O'Reilly. Her knees are giving her gyp again. Swollen ankles too.'

'Sorry to hear that. It's the weather, I expect. Well, off to see the wizard.'

Reg looked quizzically at her.

'Off to see the wizard, the wonderful wizard of Oz. I was a Munchkin. Scarborough, it was. I won't say how long ago. Horrible costumes. Green tights.'

Malcolm held the car door for her, then walked around to get in.

'Aren't you going to shut your front door, Mr O'Reilly?' said Reg.

Malcolm O'Reilly turned, sighed, and went back to the house to close the door. It seemed different rules on first names applied to females.

Graham was out of breath as they walked up the cobbled slope to the mighty door, towering two floors high, with a smaller door set inside it. This Dario chap was walking far too fast for him, chatting animatedly to Giles and Francesca. The hotel had had a proper breakfast buffet for a change. Perhaps that was because the clientele was mainly American, and he was replete with bacon, fried eggs, hash browns (a novelty) and an outsize tomato. The sausage had been far too spicy, and the stack of pancakes with maple syrup were sitting heavily. What a strange thing to serve with breakfast!

At the buffet, a man in the most garish pink and lime green shirt covered with palm trees and pineapples had asked him which state he was from. How intrusive. He had replied England, and the man had turned to his wife, 'I thought so. Boston,' then turned back, 'New Joisy. Atlantic City.'

Graham had nodded. Correcting the perceived New England to England would only have extended an unwelcome conversation.

'This was a *palazzo*, during the Kingdom of Two Sicilies,' Dario explained, then pointed at the brass plate with the small union flag above it, 'Now British Council,' he lowered his voice, 'This is important. They do too much teacher training. Today we shall see local trainers and opinion makers from the wide region. Some were at yesterday, but not all. Mainly it will be the discussion.'

They stepped over the base of the inset door. The floor beyond was stone flags. The ceilings were high above them. The dank stone was crumbling on the sides. It looked dilapidated. Dario pressed an intercom on a metal internal door, and they walked through to a bright modern reception area with light oak walls and posters of red telephone boxes, Big Ben, Windsor Castle and a policeman in helmet directing traffic. Book display shelves lined the walls. Graham noted glossy brochures for World English Centre, Euro-Lang, International House and Bell School on a shelf. 'This is the library,' Dario explained. A woman came from a side door and they conversed in Italian. Dario nodded. 'We will prepare,' he said, 'We shall set the book display for UUP. It will take some time. This lady says the Council Officer will entertain you,' he smiled, 'He is very interesting man.'

· · ·

Graham was led through to an office, along a corridor festooned with even more posters. Tower Bridge. Concorde in flight. Stonehenge. The Beatles crossing Abbey Road. Westminster Abbey. A burly man in a crumpled white linen jacket and a fraying college tie stood to greet him.

'Donaldson? Delighted to meet you, old chap. Gordon Glendower. British Council, come in, come in. Sit down, sit down. Tea? Coffee,' the man looked at his watch, 'Virtually eleven. Perhaps we'll nip downstairs to the local bar instead. Sun must be over the yardarm somewhere or other.'

The man stood up, and beckoned Graham to follow outside.

'Leave the troops to unpack. Officers and gentlemen, time for a beer,' he grinned, 'Authors count as gentlemen in the mess. May I call you Graham? Thank you. Do call me Gordon. Chaps at school called me Gee Gee …' he caught Graham's bewildered look, 'Gee Gee. Gordon Glendower. Fondness for the fillies. Partial to a wager too.'

Graham remembered Giles' exhortations to make friendly conversation, 'Um, I see. Have you been here long?'

'Nearly two years. Learning the language, though I still tend to say *Gracias* instead of *Grazie*.'

'Which part of England are you from?' said Graham. Perhaps he was getting the hang of this social interaction business.

'England! Good Lord, no. I'm a Taffy.' Gordon had an Advanced RP English accent. Definitely public school, 'I'm Welsh as they come. You should see me at Cardiff Arms Park for the rugger, belting out *Land of My Fathers*. Had a trial for Glamorgan. County Cricket. Spin bowler.'

The bar was only fifty yards away. It was tiny, and the inhabitants were in dusty working clothes. Gordon stood at the counter.

'Beer? No? What then?'

'Just a coffee,' said Graham.

'Shouldn't be here, really. *Carabiniere* popped by the Council yesterday,' he laughed, 'Said I was on a target list. Keep away from public places. Possibility of kidnapping,' he mused, 'Finger in a matchbox stuff. Or bombing I suppose, or shooting.'

Graham blanched and looked round the tiny bar. Rough types all of them. Thuggish-looking. Unshaven. All of them were smoking. 'Mafia?' he ventured.

'No, no. Political. Terrorists. Couldn't make head nor tail whether it was neo-fascists or communists. Either. Or both. Anti-British whatever.'

Graham gulped, 'Are we safe here?'

'As much as anywhere. This is a soft posting for me. I've had Bulgaria, then Libya. Language was a bastard in both. Couple of years in Saigon. Then Argentina ... we promote Welsh language down there. Did you know? Patagonia's full of Taffies. Marvellous place. Up to Paraguay ... that's why I keep saying *Gracias* instead of *Grazie*. No, Naples is a doddle. Splendid city.'

Graham kept glancing at the door.

'Thing is they imagine we're all spooks. Spies,' Gordon reflected, 'No doubt some of my colleagues were. Certainly in Bulgaria and Tripoli. Not me. Nearly got in deep doo-doo in Paraguay once. Road block. Jungle road. Whether they were guerrillas or merely bandits, who knows? Festooned with gun belts. I was driving a chap who'd just arrived. Lieutenant-Commodore. "Drive on!" he said, pulled down the window and shot two of the blighters with his service pistol. Naval attaché. Odd.'

Graham swallowed, 'Odd?'

'Paraguay's landlocked. Often wondered why the Embassy needed a naval attaché. James Bond was a naval officer. 007. In the books.'

Graham had never read the books nor seen the films.

Gordon drained his glass, '*Tempus fugit*. Back on our heads,' he noted Graham's furrowed brow, 'Back on our heads? Old joke.'

'I don't know it.'

'Must have heard it. Chap dies. Goes to hell. Probably a politician. The devil leads him into a room. Lots of fellows standing waist deep in excrement, drinking cups of tea. Chap thinks hell doesn't seem too bad, then the devil claps his hands, "Tea break over. Back on your heads,"' he paused, 'Meaning standing on their heads.'

Graham wondered, not for the first time, why so many jokes were not funny.

They left the bar and turned back towards the palazzo. Graham looked cautiously from side to side, expecting kidnappers or terrorists at every turn,

Suddenly there was a loud bang right behind them. Graham started. Did you hear the bang before the bullet hit you or vice versa? Speed of sound versus speed of bullet.

Gordon Glendower roared with laughter, 'Vespa backfiring. By the look on your face I was worried you'd backfired too. You've gone as white as a sheet.'

They turned into the palazzo, 'They'll be ready for us now. Gorgeous fillies most of them. A couple look like Gina Lollobrigida. Wish I were ten years younger. You'll see what I mean. My staff too. Brits. Teachers here and trainers. Considerably less attractive than the Italians.'

The large room had been set up with a semi-circle of chairs with two seats in the middle for Graham and Gordon. There were thirty teachers in there, nearly all of them were women. Giles was chatting to a couple of women in the front row. A book display was against the back wall, where Dario and Francesca were sitting. Graham hovered while Gordon kissed cheeks and hugged around the room. The fellow seemed to be making the most of the hugging and squeezing too. Giles may have had a point about sartorial matters. It was clear that the scruffy group of five at one side, three women, two men, were the British.

Gordon came back to the centre, 'We'd like to welcome Dr Graham Donaldson, who is in Italy on a British Council teacher training tour before the Rome conference tomorrow...'

Graham was startled. What was the man talking about? This was the first and last British Council talk of the tour. No doubt trying to take credit for bringing him here. Teacher training? He had only expected to talk about his book and grammar, surely?

'As you know, we are strictly non-commercial,' said Gordon, 'Though we have invited United Universities Press to display their latest titles, which you are free to examine in the coffee break. Dr Donaldson will not be talking about his textbook, but will be discussing the role of theories of grammar with you, and we very much hope this will be a two-way discussion, not a lecture nor a book promotion.'

Giles was seated at the end of the front row. What a swine! The British Council had paid nothing for the trip, nor expenses but were now not only claiming all credit, but preventing Graham mentioning his book. Dario had warned them that this was likely, but said it didn't matter. Being there was enough. The secretary had been most difficult about the brochures for *Intercourse* and for WEC Training Courses which Giles had placed on every seat. 'We do not favour any UK school over any other,' she had told him sharply. Francesca had interrupted and pointed out that UUP were meeting all expenses and WEC had allowed the time off work, and the brochures were part of the agreement. To Dario's horror, Francesca had continued, 'Or of course we could just leave now.' The woman had backed down. Dario made a mental note to send her a bunch of flowers as a thank you, or rather an apology. He could easily blame the absent Florentine once Francesca had gone. Dario also knew that was what Francesca would expect him to do.

At that point, Francesca leaned over and whispered, 'Don't invite the bastard to lunch.'

'He will expect it,' said Dario.

'He will be disappointed,' she finished, 'I don't like him.'

The questions were going well. Mostly they were on points of grammar and whether grammar explanation should be explicit or implicit. It was all safe ground for Graham. The Brits were surprisingly quiet, though Giles noted the folded arms and tight-lipped surly expressions.

A woman put her hand up. She had long black curly hair a pouting mouth and low cleavage. Graham was trying hard to remember who Gina Lollobrigida was. Possibly this is what the loud and coarse fellow had meant.

'*Professore* Argento. *Prego* ...' said Gordon Glendower

'Please, *dottore,*' she said, 'I have question about your book ...'

'Well, we're not here to discuss commercial textbooks...' started Gordon.

'I'm happy to answer,' said Graham loudly, 'Please continue, er, professor.' He could almost feel Glendower's glare.

'Yes. Thank you. So, I am use your book *Passports* and I have problem with this new functional method.'

'Er, *Passports* is not by me,' said Graham, 'In fact, I believe that's Truman Education, not UUP.'

'I thought this was from you,' she said, 'I apologise. I was going to say my students do not like this method. So before we have lesson on prepositions of place and adverbs of movement and students ask for the directions. Now we have new title 'Asking for Directions.' Is not different lesson. Is same. So please what is your book, *dottore?*'

'*Intercourse,*' said Graham, 'In fact there are brochures on your seats ...'

'Please. I wish to know more from this book and in which ways it differs from *Passports*...'

There were nods all around the audience, although not, he noticed, from the British contingent.

Francesca leaned over to Dario, 'You know *Professore* Argento, I think.'

'My sister-in-law,' whispered Dario, 'I was prepared for the non-commercial talk. *Passports* is our main opposition.'

'I know. Our sales director in England, Patrick, calls it Pisspots.'

'Which way is the check-in counter?' said Gloria.

'I'm sure there will be signs. We don't need to ask for directions,' Malcolm replied.

Reg was muttering as he loaded the suitcases and boxes of brochures onto the luggage trolley. Was that an under-the-breath, 'I'm not a fucking porter,' that Malcolm had heard? Best to ignore it.

'You wanna watch you don't get a hernia, Mr O'Reilly,' Reg stretched, 'Ouch. I think I might of.'

'Might have,' said Malcolm automatically, 'So, we'll see you on Monday morning.'

'I'll have to get up at the crack of dawn,' complained Reg.

'Ten-thirty arrival?' said Malcolm, 'Hardly. It'll take us a while to collect our luggage and get through. I'm sure eleven would be perfectly sufficient. We won't be bringing the brochures back either.' Then the thought struck him. Say Graham Donaldson was on the same Monday morning flight from Rome? They would surely be obliged to offer him a lift back to Bournemouth.

It had been a good while since Malcolm and Gloria had taken a scheduled flight, rather than the travel agency arranged holiday trips from Bournemouth airport. It gave Malcolm O'Reilly a sense of importance as they pushed the trolley through to check in. It was most cosmopolitan. Two Hare Krishna men in orange robes with shaven heads were walking past a group of Hassidic Jews with their tall black hats and ringlets. Two women dressed entirely in black with burqas were leading a procession of tired looking Filipinos pushing luggage trolleys piled high with trunks. Two more Filipinas were leading a small group of children at the end of the procession. Malcolm O'Reilly spotted the Rome check-in line before he read the notice. Half of the check-in queue were either priests or nuns. They joined the end.

Gloria nudged, 'At least if the plane crashes we'll be alright for the last rites,' she said. She had always had a loud, or perhaps piercing, stage whisper.

Two elderly clerics looked round. They were not smiling. O'Reilly nodded politely.

'It's the nuns that terrify me,' Gloria continued.

'They appear most benign,' said Malcolm as quietly as he could.

'You didn't go to a Catholic school,' she said.

'Neither did you,' Malcolm replied.

'Yes, I did. Didn't I tell you? Only for a year. I got expelled. Anyway, a lot of my friends did.' Her voice was too loud for Malcolm's liking.

'Reminds me of a joke,' said Gloria, and giggled, 'This girl Bridey, at a St Mary's Covent goes to see the headmistress, who was also the Mother Superior ...'

Malcolm wondered how he could discreetly stop her.

'So the Mother Superior says, "What are you after doing when you leave the school, Bridey, my child?"'

The stage Irish accent was drawing more attention from the priests in front. O'Reilly knew the joke too.

'Anyway, Bridey pipes up, "I want to be a prostitute, mother." The Mother Superior falls to the floor in a dead faint. Other nuns rush in with smelling salts and holy water and revive her. "What did you say, Bridey," gasps the Mother Superior. "I want to be a prostitute," says Bridey. "Thank Christ for that," says the Mother Superior, "I thought you said you wanted to be a Protestant!"'

Malcolm O'Reilly felt the flush in his cheeks. They edged forward. One of the priests turned round. What was he going to say?

The priest smiled, 'Actually that was quite funny. It's a very old joke, but you told it well. Are you going to Rome?'

'Puttanesca. Prostitute's sauce or pizza,' said Dario, 'It was named because the prostitutes would eat it to maintain their energy, or the alternate, would use the salty and hot aroma to attract the clients. It has capers, olives, chilli and anchovies.'

Francesca shook her head firmly, 'I think prostitute is too technical. Too modern. For the 18th century in Naples, whore is better. Whore's pizza. Do you think this is a better choice of word, Giles?'

'Given the historical context,' Giles started cautiously, 'It would fit better in a play or novel about a past era. As in *'Tis Pity She's A Whore* ... the play.'

'They also suggest that the anchovies have the smell of fish, as did the whores,' continued Francesca, 'But this is somewhat vulgar. So Graham, will you try a Puttanesca?

Francesca had insisted they have a genuine Neapolitan pizza before catching their train to Rome, and Dario had declared that the massive and noisy pizza restaurant at the harbour was the most authentic.

Francesca noted Graham's expression, 'Or the classic Pizza Margherita. This will demonstrate the basic ingredients best ... the

San Marzano tomatoes and buffalo mozzarella and fresh basil. The legend is that it was invented in 1889 in honour of Queen Margherita of Savoy, who was then Queen of all of Italy. So we have the red of tomato, the white of mozzarella and the green of basil.'

'The colour of the Italian flag,' put in Dario, 'In Naples we question the story. These ... foods?'

'Ingredients,' said Francesca.

'These ingredients were always here.'

'Yes, yes,' said Graham, 'I'll have that one. The plainer one. The Margaret.'

Graham looked at them glumly. It seemed these people nattered interminably about either food, history or preferably both together. He'd had to endure far too much of it on the hair-raising drive in heavy traffic past Pompeii and Herculaneum, then everyone had scoffed at him when he had simply enquired whether Mount Vesuvius was quite safe to drive past. Having listened to Francesca and Giles droning on about the famous eruption in Roman times, it had seemed a reasonable query. Then after a tiring one hour session with teachers in Sorrento, Dario had driven them along the coast road to Amalfi to admire the view. Graham had felt quite nauseous what with the bends and the sheer drop, and that was aggravated by Giles' constant exclamations of delight. Graham had wanted to say 'Yes, the sea is blue. What did you expect?' Teachers from all along the Amalfi coast had attended his talk, and one had to admit that the standard of English was higher than elsewhere, which Dario had explained was a result of the high numbers of English tourists. The literary showing-off had been emphasized when the third teacher mentioned that *Duchess of Malfi* play. It was apparently a popular choice in literature classes in the area. He had struggled to avoid admitting that he had no idea of either the plot or the history. He had also forgotten who wrote it.

Graham's reverie was interrupted by laughter from his companions. He looked up.

'That's very clever, Giles,' Francesca was saying.

'Very good joke,' said Dario.

'What?' snapped Graham.

'Didn't you hear? Giles has suggested that the best translation of Pizza Puttanesca was A Tart's Tart.'

'I find that rather coarse,' said Graham.

'Rather better than a Stale's Stale ...' laughed Giles, then seeing the lack of comprehension, added, 'A stale in Shakespeare was a lady of easy virtue ... um, a woman of the night. Also you would not want to advertise pastry as stale. I suppose the word origin relates to lack of freshness ...'

'Excuse me,' said Graham, 'Could you direct me to the gentlemen's toilets?' He stood up. Not that he would ever be able to empty his bowels in a public facility. Things had definitely closed off there since the dramatic olive oil soup event. The bottle of oil was currently sitting at the side of Dario's car's boot, held upright by boxes of books. It was more that he preferred to avoid the unsavoury direction the conversation was taking. Who would have thought an editor at United Universities Press would see fit to entertain foreigners with vulgarity? As he moved away he heard Giles again.

'There are pros and cons with pros ...'

The fellow had obviously imbibed too freely from the large carafe of red wine.

***

Malcolm O'Reilly took the room key, 'Thank you so very much,' he said, '*Grazie mille.*'

'*Prego,*' the receptionist replied with a wide smile, 'You are welcome, sir. And welcome to Rome.'

'*Prego,*' he said, inclining his head, 'I must compliment you on your command of English. I am the principal of a major language school in England.'

'Where is that, sir?'

'Bournemouth,' said Malcolm, looking quickly at her name badge, 'Do you know it, Bianca?'

'Very well,' she said, 'I attend the Euro-Lang school there. For two month.'

Malcolm managed to maintain his smile, 'Well, they taught you very well. I am at World English Centre.'

'Ah, I know this. I stayed in Capstone Road. I walk past every day. It is beautiful school. But too expensive for me.'

'What a small world it is. You must remember Mr Arnold at Euro-Lang?'

'Ah, yes. He did not teach often my class. He was boring.'

Malcolm smiled in triumph.

'Oh, I am very sorry! I am too rude. He must be your good friend!' said Bianca.

"Not at all. I agree with you completely,' he said, 'He is unfortunately rather boring.'

She laughed, 'It is a pleasure to meet you. If you need anything at this hotel or you have problem, ask for me, Bianca.'

'*Molte grazie*, Bianca,' he said.

Malcolm O'Reilly reflected on his knack of getting on with foreigners. Perhaps it was a combination of an imposing stance, clarity of diction and a natural gift for courtesy. He had arranged to leave the two boxes of brochures downstairs in the luggage storeroom, which had earned him a degree of gratitude from the porter.

Gloria was waiting for him, 'What are you doing chatting up that young girl, Malkie,' she said, 'You're old enough to be her father.'

'Obviously. I was merely arranging to store the brochures. She studied English in Bournemouth, you know. At Euro-Lang. What a coincidence.'

'Well, you be careful. They prey on older men some of these girls. Appeal to their vanity.'

Malcolm frowned at the accusation. Vanity? Him?

Gloria looked round the lobby, 'It's quite posh in here,' she said, 'And no one's pinched my bum yet.' She sounded disappointed. 'I wonder what the restaurant's like.'

'I believe we should follow Lorenzo's advice,' said Malcolm, 'He suggested we try a restaurant not far from the Roman Forum. He travels to Rome often on business, and said we would find few if any tourists there.'

'Will you have to speak Italian, Malkie?' she said, 'They all speak English here in the hotel.'

'I shall cope. I'm sure it will be better food than the hotel.'

'Do you remember that trattoria in Weston-Super-Mare? When we were doing that *Dry Rot* tour? We ate there every night.'

Malcolm remembered it well. While they may have eaten there every night, it had meant steak and chips six times for Gloria. 'There was not a great deal of choice in Weston,' he said, 'And they opened early.'

'That waiter was a greasy bugger. You know he followed Cheryl right into the Ladies on the Saturday night after the last performance? Tried it on by the washbasins?'

Malcolm had heard the story many times, not least from Cheryl, 'I do recall him. Hirsute fellow. In fact he was not Italian. He was from Kidderminster, I believe.'

'Arms like an orang-utang. That's what she said. Bent her right over into the taps. And Cheryl was never prissy. She smacked him right round the chops. Just because you're an actress they think you're up for it.'

There were four seats together. Francesca led them to the seats, and Giles put Graham's luggage and that bottle of olive oil on the rack.

'It is not a long journey,' said Francesca, 'and at least we have the seats.'

'Signorina Garibaldi! And Doctor Donaldson! How fortunate I am! May I join you?'

'Of course,' said Francesca. The woman standing there was in her late thirties, beautifully dressed. 'You all remember Signora Pellegrino from Positano? She was at your talk in Sorrento today.'

Giles immediately stood up, 'Giles Winthrop,' he said, 'I'm Mr Donaldson's editor at UUP.'

'Congratulations. You have made a very good book,' she said.

'Thank you.'

Graham stayed put, and glared up. What was Giles doing accepting thanks for his work? Pellegrino? He thought of the bottle of mineral water the Garibaldi women kept ordering. San Pellegrino. Were they all named after food and drink? It seemed likely. 'Like the water?' he blurted out.

Francesca looked at him rather strangely he thought, 'Like the saint. In English, he was called St Peregrine. He was from Forli and lived in the thirteenth and fourteenth century. His name means 'pilgrim' which is also an English surname, I believe.'

The interminable history, thought Graham. Did they never tire of it?

'So my pilgrimage to Rome begins,' said the woman, 'Please call me Claudia. I am going to the conference, like you … yourselves.'

'I am a pilgrim and a stranger travelling through this wearisome land,' said Giles.

There was silence.

'Um, it's a song. By The Byrds? From *Sweetheart of The Rodeo*?' he stuttered.

'I don't know this,' said Francesca.

'Nor I,' said Claudia.

Graham just grunted.

'Not that this is a wearisome land. Not in the slightest. Absolutely delightful, in fact. Let me put your bag on the rack,' said Giles hurriedly, 'I'm so sorry. Songs just come into my head. Doesn't it ever happen to you?'

'No,' said Graham.

Claudia sat opposite Graham, 'I am so lucky. I am in charge of the teacher training course in Sorrento. I was very interested in your description of conditionals this afternoon. I should love to discuss this further with you.'

Graham glanced at Giles and Francesca. They were ignoring him and conversing about the damned ... or rather blessed ... saint and places of pilgrimage.

'*The Canterbury Tales* is the template,' Giles was saying.

They were not about to rescue him.

"Now please explain how or why the subjunctive form is disappearing ... ' continued Claudia.

Francesca led them to the taxi queue. Giles had remembered the blasted olive oil too, but at least he was carrying it. Claudia had been met at the station by her cousin. Graham found the hug and peck on both cheeks most embarrassing, but on reflection, the journey had passed well. Claudia had proven erudite and a good listener. She had almost cried with laughter when Graham had said, 'If I were you, I would allow students to say "If he was in the army ..." and "If she was a nurse ..."' though he was rather shocked when she responded that his choice of pronouns reinforced gender stereotypes. At least it had been more interesting than listening to Winthrop and the Garibaldi woman wittering on about Santiago de Compostela. When they had tried to draw him and Claudia into the conversation, he had asked which part of Italy it was in, and he had found their amusement most insulting. How was he to know they were talking about Spain?

Francesca looked at the row of grubby Fiat 124s edging their way into the line at the rank, 'You will soon see that the Romans are lazy people and this is why they are unpopular in other parts of Italy. They are idle. This is because Rome had Barbarian invasions from all. The Goths, the Vandals, the Burgundians, the French, everyone destroyed the city ...'

'Sacked the city,' said Giles.

'Thank you, Giles. Now I remember this word. The noble Roman of myth has long since departed. None are left here. These people are not descended from Julius Caesar, the noblest Roman of them all,' she paused, pleased with herself, 'As Shakespeare said.'

'Actually Brutus was the noblest Roman of them all, not Caesar ... er, it's in Mark Antony's speech. Don't you think it was sarcasm, in fact? Mark Antony didn't mean it.'

Graham had known that these people only discussed food, history and literature. It was confirmed. Francesca was looking most disgruntled. Disgruntled. A good word. He must note it.

'English public schools in the nineteenth century believed that the true Romans had ended up in England,' said Giles.

Francesca laughed scornfully, 'I really do not think so,' she said.

'Nor do I, but some old public school masters in dusty gowns thought so. After all, the Romans were in Britain for four hundred years. Aren't most capital cities disliked by the rest of the country? The same happens with London and Paris.'

'But in Rome it is true,' said Francesca firmly, 'Watch.'

They were at the head of the line. The taxi driver was short and dark with two or three days' stubble. He stared at their bags, groaned, and opened the boot. Then he got back in the driver's seat.

'You see? He expects us to load the bags by ourselves.'

'I'll do it,' said Giles promptly. He put the bags in, held the doors open for Graham and Francesca and got in the front seat. Graham coughed. The driver was smoking and the radio was loud, playing some dreadful Italian song.

Francesca gave the hotel name. 'You see?' she said to Graham.

After a ten minute very bumpy journey in heavy traffic, the taxi pulled up at the side of the road and the driver spoke to Francesca. She replied in voluble Italian. The driver put his hands out and shook his head.

'Madonna!' she said, 'This one is worse than I thought. He wants us to get out here, because it is only two hundred metres to walk across the piazza, but a long way round the one way system to the door. I have pointed out that we have luggage and it is starting to rain, but he doesn't want to drive all the way round to the hotel in the traffic.'

'He'll get a larger fare!' exclaimed Giles.

'I don't think money is an incentive,' she replied.

The driver had got out and opened the boot. He stood and watched as Giles unloaded. Graham had rather hoped he might forget the olive oil, but it was not to be.

Francesca paid. The driver said something, and she gave him another high speed burst of Italian. She turned to the two men, 'He asks why there is no tip.'

She spoke again. The driver just shrugged, got in and drove away in a cloud of blue exhaust smoke.

'We must walk,' she said.

It had been a splendid meal, and Malcolm O'Reilly was replete. The taxi dropped them right at the hotel steps, and they strolled into the lobby. A pleasant driver. Not much English but he had appreciated Malcolm's attempts at Italian phrases. It had been pleasant recalling their theatrical days over the meal, and they had stuck to just a litre of wine plus the free grappa which had arrived with the bill. It was new to both of them.

'Let's have a nightcap, Malkie,' said Gloria who'd spotted the hotel bar, 'We are on holiday after all.'

'Actually we're on business,' said Malcolm, 'And we had one in the restaurant.'

'Still, a gin and tonic would help us sleep.'

'I rather think tonic would have the reverse effect,' he said, but then he relented, 'I suppose we could. It's been a long day.'

They walked into the bar. Malcolm immediately noticed the group of four at the table by the door.

'Good Lord!' he said, 'Graham Donaldson!'

Graham looked round in horror, 'O'Reilly!'

'Hello, Graham,' said Gloria, 'Long time no see. Which one's your girlfriend?' she smiled, 'They're both very lovely. That one's much too young. Both out of your league, I'd've thought. Hello, dears. I'm Gloria. Gloria O'Reilly now. On stage I was Gloria Galore, but that was long before your time.'

Giles got to his feet. Graham was beginning to find this constant leaping up and down by Winthrop on all occasions most irritating. He thought it quite obsequious.

'Giles Winthrop,' UUP,' he said, 'You must be Mr O'Reilly from WEC. I heard you were coming.'

'Malcolm,' he replied, 'So pleased to meet you, Giles,' he looked down at the open-mouthed Graham, 'Aren't you going to introduce your companions, Graham?'

Francesca was already standing, 'Francesca Garibaldi from UUP, Italia. So you're Graham's boss?'

'Indeed I am,' said Malcolm.

Luciana didn't stand, but gave a little wave, 'Hello. I'm Luciana. I work for UUP too. More of a dogsbody, me. She's my boss.'

'We'd be honoured if you joined us,' said Giles, 'Now let me get you both a drink? What are you having?'

'I do like him,' said Gloria, 'He's got the right idea. G & T for me, darling. Best make it a double. Ice and lemon,' she looked round the table, 'I'll sit next to you, sweetheart,' she said to Luciana, 'You can tell me about your nose stud. Very attractive. Is it silver? What's it like when you've got a cold? I've always wondered, with the snot and that.'

Luciana shifted along the bench seat to let her in, 'So you were an actress?' she said.

'After I met Malkie. More of a hoofer before. Hoofer? Dancer? Where are you from, luv?'

'Blackpool,' said Luciana.

'Blackpool! I thought so. Never miss an accent. I could tell you some tales. I did three summer shows there.'

'What are you doing at the same hotel?' snapped Graham suddenly. Of course he had expected to see O'Reilly at some point. The fellow had told him often enough of his plans to exploit ... no, piggyback on ... Graham's Rome conference exposure with UUP. He had not expected to have to socialise with the man. Now here Graham was vainly attempting to relax after a most tiring and tiresome day and then O'Reilly and his loud and loathsome wife had arrived and butted in. He shuddered at her leering comments to him regarding the women at the table. No doubt she believed she was being facetious.

'It is one of the recommended hotels for the conference,' said Malcolm, 'So hardly surprising or a coincidence. I do trust you've had a rewarding tour, Graham.'

Graham woke early. He'd gone to bed seething with indignation after O'Reilly's repeated reminders that Graham was in fact, an employee and that he, the mighty Malcolm O'Reilly, was his Director of Studies. This Roman bedroom felt cramped after the vast expanses of the Naples room, and much as he'd sneered at the ornate gold taps and was nervous of the alarmingly large floor to ceiling window of the Neapolitan hotel, this one was rather plain and gloomy, missing the space, light and overt luxury. The day loomed ahead. The first of his two talks was at five, and that Garibaldi woman had said he should spend some time on the bookstand speaking to teachers, just as if he were a shop assistant in a book shop. He sat on the bed staring at the infernal bag with the olive oil. It was hard to believe that anyone thought such an item worth transporting hundreds, if not thousands of miles. Then they'd had to spend time, risking their lives no doubt, delivering the other bottle to a Neapolitan restaurant full of gangsters ... Gangsters. Criminals. Bandits. Crooks. Hoodlums. Mobsters. Desperados. Outlaws. A den of thieves. What had the Italian woman said? Ah, yes. Mafiosi. He struggled, this would be worth a note in his next book. What did they want with olive oil? Possibly oiling their guns. Revolvers. Pistols. 38s. Peacemakers. Rifles. Machine ... no,

Tommy guns. Graham took his pen and sat down at the small table with his notebook.

Gloria sank the double espresso in one gulp, and spread some jam on the croissant, 'I needed that coffee, Malkie. Bit of a head. Lovely girl, that Luciana. Good sense of humour. I said I was calling her Lucy from now on, none of that foreign stuff. She said her bitch of a maths teacher used to do the same so she went and complained to the headmistress that it was racial discrimination ... she's half Itie, you know. Feisty. Just the sort of daughter I'd imagined having.' Gloria stared wistfully through the restaurant window.

'Somewhat extreme in the fashion sense,' ventured Malcolm, 'One fears the next step might be young women with bones sticking through their noses.'

'Oh, they're all like that now. It's this punk thing. I'd have a nose stud like a shot if I was her age.'

'Nevertheless,' said Malcolm. One of his tasks on return would be revising the sartorial guidelines for World English Centre teachers for next year. In spite of a hot summer earlier in the year, he had declined to lift his ban on shorts and on sandals for male teachers. He supposed he would have to adjudicate on the questions of earrings and ear studs for males, and heaven forbid, nose studs for females. He would certainly draw the line well before metal stuck in lips or cheeks or eyebrows. Safety pins definitely not. However, they relied on recent graduates for summer course teaching, so perhaps a little flexibility would be necessary. After all, if nose studs for staff members were acceptable to such an august publisher as UUP, it might be unstoppable. Then there was the question of hair colour, let alone extreme hair styles.

Francesca walked round the stand for the third time. UUP had five tables, the biggest stand in the book exhibition hall. She moved one book a centimetre to the left and its neighbour to the right on the display stand, and leaned back to check, 'Very good, Luciana.'

'Should be. It took me all bloody evening,' said Luciana, 'Those blokes from the Rome office are idle bastards. Stood and watched me mainly. I expect it was because I had to keep bending over in a short skirt. Dirty sods.'

Copies of *Intercourse* filled the centre, along with the Teacher's Book and cassette cases.

'The cassette cases are empty, I hope?' said Francesca.

'Course. I'm not daft. They had all the cassettes away from the stand in Bologna. Teachers'll nick anything, then pretend they thought they were on offer. That's why there's only one teacher's book up there. I've got a box of more under the table.'

'We can give them free to decision makers,' said Francesca, 'But do it discretely, or everyone around will ask for one.'

'Yeah, then I have to tell them they're not important enough for a freebie.' Luciana reflected, 'I'd quite like that.'

'The "speakers at this conference" display is most important,' Francesca said. UUP had a pre-printed folded strip to put on covers for the purpose. 'Even if they're Applied Linguistics and we don't sell any. They give us prestige and if they're not on display the authors all complain to Head Office.'

'You told me.'

Francesca scanned the display, 'What about Sirio Ubaldini's book?'

'It's on the side table over there. Really? It's not only over twenty years old, it's total bloody crap. Even the cover's boring.'

'He's on the conference committee. Put it with the others.'

Lucina sighed, 'The unreadables. Have you ever tried to read it?'

'Ubaldini is both miserable and pompous too,' said Francesca, 'He believes he is a great intellectual. But we have to do it.'

'Alright.'

'I've just had an idea. When Mr O'Reilly appears, take him a couple of copies of *Intercourse* and some "Speaker at this conference" signs.'

'You reckon? Gloria was saying O'Reilly hates Graham's guts. Well, she put it a bit stronger than that. She called Graham a right C-word.'

'It will be to his advantage. It will draw attention to his brochures for World English Centre.'

It hadn't looked far at all on the map the hotel had given him, and Giles was looking forward to walking, and getting some fresh air, and quite frankly, some time on his own. He was not used to company for every meal of the day and in between too. While he relished his conversations with Francesca, the increasingly grumpier Graham was beginning to get on his nerves.

Giles had foolishly imagined Rome to be bathed in eternal sunshine, but at this time of year the fog was just beginning to lift from the streets. The cobbles were uncomfortable underfoot too, but every corner, every alley, every street, held magic in his eyes. Another Bob Dylan line, 'The streets of Rome are filled with rubble. Ancient footprints are everywhere.' The song, *When I Paint My Masterpiece*, started playing in his head. As the conference was in a seminary next to the Vatican, he hardly needed the map. St. Peter's dome loomed a short distance away.

He would have to put up with Graham whining. Giles had managed to avoid him at breakfast, but had bumped into him on the way out of the restaurant. Giles had cheerily announced that he was going to walk to the conference. Graham had said he wasn't ready to leave yet, and when he was, he would prefer to travel in a taxi. Perhaps 'Yes, you do that, Graham,' had not been sufficiently placatory. Graham's 'What? Travel alone!' had been agonised.

'How kind, Luciana,' said Malcolm O'Reilly, placing the books in an emerald green cardboard book holder in the centre of the single exhibition table he'd reserved. Luciana had brought him the book holder too, and the prominent gold UUP logo should add to WEC's image.

'Any time, er ...' Luciana considered. Gloria had only ever referred to him as Malkie. She couldn't. It might be a pet name, 'Er, Mr O'Reilly.'

'Malcolm, please, my dear.'

'If you go for a coffee or nip off to the loo, bung them under the table. Teachers will nick any books at a conference.'

'I will. I can put them under some brochures in the box.'

'Oh, yeah. You haven't got a table cloth. We always cover the table right down to the floor at these things so we can put stuff out of sight. I'll bring a spare UUP one. You can put it on with the logo at the back.'

'I'm most indebted.'

'Is Gloria coming to the conference?'

'Alas no,' he said, 'I've booked her on a full day tour of Rome including a three course lunch. She should enjoy it. The rest of the party appears to be entirely American, and they are generally friendly and gregarious people in my experience.'

'I bet they didn't say that in Vietnam,' Luciana said.

'Indeed not, but in the context of a sightseeing tour on holiday ... or rather vacation ... Americans are generally easy to get along with.'

'S'pose,' she said, 'I'd better get over to the hotel and walk Graham Donaldson back here. Giles said he was put out at being "abandoned" as he put it. So Francesca telephoned his room and offered my services as an escort, though not in the tacky sense of the word, thank Christ. I think she must have got him off the bog or something. He was even more bad-tempered than normal.'

'Thank you again, Luciana.' Malcolm smiled at the mental image

of Graham trotting along behind the bovver-booted and spiky-haired
Luciana. A most attractive young lady. Not that Graham would be
likely to notice. He might re-word the passage on jewellery for female
staff. He was getting used to the nose stud.

'I just need to go back to my room,' said Graham testily, 'Wait here.'

'Best be quick about it. I'll get an earful from Francesca if I'm
away from the stand too long,' said Luciana. Why a grown man
needed an escort for the short walk was beyond belief.

'What?' Graham was appalled that such a ridiculously attired
female junior employee should see fit to give him instructions. After
earlier interrupted efforts ... that phone call ... had produced stools
the size of peas, he had thought he might be inspired to try again.

'You're the author,' she said, 'Take your time. Don't worry about
it. It's me that'll get the bollocking.'

Graham gave a loud 'huff!' and walked back to the lift. All desire
had left him. Still, worth a try. He wondered momentarily about a
spoonful of the olive oil, but would he ever get the cork back in? Or in
a physiological sense, the cork back out?

Gloria had managed to grab the window seat. Thankfully, as the
woman's extensive girth meant she would protrude several inches
into the gangway.

'Kansas City, you say?' Gloria started, '12th Street and Vine?'

'Pardon Me?' said Mavis. They had exchanged names before
boarding, and Gloria had nipped up the steps first.

Gloria sang, '*Standing on the corner, 12th Street and Vine?* The
song? Kansas City?'

'That neighbourhood has been demolished,' said Mavis, 'It no
longer exists fortunately,' she leaned close and whispered, 'Jazz clubs

and, well, we used to call them coloured. I live in Mission Hills. Say, if you ever visit KC, Gloria, you should look me up.'

Gloria decided that a reciprocal invitation to Bournemouth might be unwise.

'Are you a widow too, hon?' enquired Mavis gently.

'No. Well, at least not yet. Not as far as I know, I haven't seen him since breakfast, so I might be. My husband's here on business.' Gloria saw that there was not a hint of a smile, so levity was not going to be appropriate.

'Eight years. Heart. My Chester dropped dead just after the third hole,' Mavis wiped her eye.

Gloria stifled the thought that Chester shouldn't have attended orgies with a bad heart. 'Golf?' she said, 'I'm very sorry.'

'He lived for golf,' said Mavis tearfully, 'Poor Chester so loved his food too. At least now he's living in eternal glory with the Lord.'

'Mmm,' said Gloria doubtfully.

'Which church do you fellowship with, hon?' asked Mavis.

'Church of England,' said Gloria instantly and automatically as she'd done throughout her life when questioned. Not that she'd been in one for decades apart from weddings and funerals.

'Episcopalian?' said Mavis. The tone of voice suggested it was akin to Satanism, 'We're strict Baptist,' she paused, 'In fact our pastor had some stern warnings about visiting Rome. He calls it Babylon and the pope the anti-Christ,' she shuddered, 'The beast ascends from the bottomless pit of perdition? Revelations 17:8.'

'Hellfire and damnation preacher?' said Gloria, 'Sounds like Burt Lancaster in that film ... what was it called? *Elmer Gantry*! I always fancied Burt Lancaster.'

'Reverend Gaylord Paisley told us all about the Jesuits and their acts of abomination. Then about the Inquisition. Stretching Protestant martyrs on the rack. Thumbscrews. Burning them alive.'

'I'm sure they're all much nicer nowadays. Popes and that. I liked that last one. He looked ever so sweet.'

Mavis frowned, 'Then the olden days Romans were pagans. They fed Christians to the lions.'

'Yes, the first stop is the Colosseum,' said Gloria, 'Malkie was telling me about that.' She had decided that she had to lose Mavis as soon as they got out at the Colosseum. What a shame there'd be no lions there now. Mavis would never outrun them. That'd be a good show. 'I played the Oldham Coliseum a couple of times on tour, that was before I met Malkie. Gorgeous leading man. A hunk. Roland was his name. I don't expect it was his real name,' Gloria giggled at the memory, 'I think he made his way through the whole chorus ... we all fancied him. Never played the London Coliseum though. Pity. It's the largest theatre in the West End, you know,' Gloria glanced down at the tour brochure and frowned, 'That's odd. Look, they spelt it wrong. C-O-L-O-S-S-E-U-M. The ones in England are all C-O-L-I-S-E-U-M. You'd think they'd know how to spell it right here.'

***

'Gabriella! My dear girl. How lovely to see you!' Malcolm O'Reilly duly kissed her on both cheeks.

'Also to see you, Mr O'Reilly,' she replied.

'Malcolm. I insist. You are to be married to one of my staff which makes you part of the WEC family.' He wondered as so often why Italian girls of intellect chose dowdy navy blue cardigans and such plain skirts. Such a shame for such a pretty girl.

Gabriella looked dubious, 'Thank you. For me, this is difficult because ... since ... I used to be your student.'

'An excellent student too. I remember, my dear. I have some books for you in the box under the table,' he continued. Weighty tomes would be more appropriate, he added mentally.

She sighed, 'I have told Barry this. I can read these in the university library. He has put you to far too much trouble.'

'No trouble at all,' he replied through gritted teeth.

'How is Barry?' she enquired.

'The same as ever. Still getting hot under the collar about politics. You know he's now the union representative?'

'He has told me. We are both committed socialists.'

Malcolm O'Reilly decided it was time to switch the topic, 'How is your course at Bologna?'

'It is nearly complete. My tutor is Dottore Sirio Ubaldini. Do you know? He is very famous ... famed? Renowned?... linguist in all of Italy.'

'Alas, no,' said O'Reilly.

'Unfortunately he has no humour, but we do not have humour in university lectures. It is not like England with always making the joking. He is too serious. He is not exciting and interesting lecturer like yourself.'

'Flattery will get you nowhere, my dear Gabriella.' O'Reilly preened. No doubt her remark was sincere.

'Always you say something funny. I like this.'

O'Reilly stooped to get the three books. Slight creak in the back. That was becoming more frequent. He brought them out and presented them.

'You were too kind for ... no, to carry them.'.'

He waved his hand dismissively, 'Not at all.'

Gabriella put a bag on the table, 'This is for you. It is a special olive oil from Emilia-Romagna. It is called *Colline de Romagna*. It is, without any question, the best olive oil in all of Italy. I must say, this is for putting bread into it, or as a salad dressing. Too good for cooking.'

'Dipping. Dipping bread,' said O'Reilly, 'How marvellous. Thank you so much, Gabriella.'

***

'Is that him?' hissed Luciana, indicating a man with a gleaming shaven head, carefully perusing the book display. He was wearing an

immaculate tweed jacket, with a pale blue cardigan and tie
beneath it.

'Yes,' whispered Francesca, 'Thank goodness you put the book
out in time.' She walked over, 'Dottore Ubaldini. Good morning.
What a pleasure to see you here. I look forward so much to your
plenary.'

'Ah, Signorina Garibaldi,' he nodded, 'I am looking. My book is
dirty.' He showed her his dusty finger.

Francesca silently cursed Luciana, along with the representatives
from the Rome office. 'This is the local office, I'm afraid,' inspiration
hit her, 'With the new semester starting so recently, they had sold a
large number,' then she realized that her lie would be revealed on his
next royalty statement. Still, since he worked in Bologna, she would
not be around when he did. 'So this will be from the office display. It
attracts the dust because it is prominent in the window.'

Ubaldini removed a spotless white handkerchief from his pocket
and wiped his finger, 'But they did not wipe this.'

'They will,' Francesca felt the glare like a blow. The obvious next
thought was that no one had ever picked it up to look inside.
'Luciana,' she called, 'This is Dottore Ubaldini. He complains that
his book is dirty.'

'Well, if you will write dirty books ...' started Luciana. No one
was smiling. 'Let me clean it for you then,' she finished, and took the
copy.

Francesca watched the scowl deepen. He had understood the
meaning of 'dirty book.' Divert his attention. Graham had just
returned from a short tour around the book exhibition and was
standing waiting expectantly for her attention. 'May I introduce
Dottore Donaldson? The author of our new course book?'

Ubaldini swivelled to glare at Graham instead.

'This is Graham Donaldson. Graham, may I introduce Sirio
Ubaldini. Sirio, this is Graham ... I am sure you two will have much
to discuss,' she finished, and scuttled back to Luciana who was at the

far end of the UUP stand, spitting vigorously onto a Kleenex tissue and wiping the cover.

Ubaldini stared at Graham, 'So. Dottore Donaldson. Signorina Garibaldi believes she may use our Christian names. Sirio! Graham! I do not like this! This is not respect!'

Luciana was on her way out of the book exhibition when she noticed Malcolm O'Reilly sitting alone at his table. He was looking puzzled. She went over, 'Hi, Malcolm.'

'Ah, Luciana. It seems virtually everyone has deserted us.'

'Yes, the thing is they'll close the book exhibition during the opening plenary speech. You won't want to get locked in.'

'Oh. I hadn't realized.'

'The etiquette is that everyone attends.'

'Of course,' O'Reilly stood up.

'You'll need your exhibitor lanyard to get in.'

O'Reilly had placed it on the table, feeling that the bright yellow rope and plastic badge card clashed so badly with his duck egg blue shirt and lilac tie. He picked it up. 'Do we actually have to wear it?' he asked.

'We do, and I am,' replied Luciana indicating her badge.

He hadn't read the conference programme, contenting himself with checking the whole page WEC advert and comparing it (favourably, after all he had designed it) with Euro-Lang and the other UK language schools. 'Who is the speaker?'

'One on our academic list. Italy only, mind. We wouldn't touch him internationally. Sirio Ubaldini. Big noise up in Bologna, so we've got to keep him sweet. Supposed to be an expert on communicative teaching. Communicative my arse! You'll see. He's a pretentious fart. Come on, let's go in.'

Malcolm O'Reilly followed her into the main hall. It was enormous, two thousand seats, Luciana had told him. The stage had a single polished oak lectern, with a massive carved and coloured statue of the crucifixion directly behind it, and it was angled forward so that it hung above the lectern at sixty degrees. It must have been thirty feet high, and the wounds were rendered in gruesome detail, the blood flowed thick and crimson. He remembered that it was a seminary. The loincloth was very low on the belly.

Giles was waving at them from about halfway back. They edged their way into the row.

'I've saved a couple of seats. Do take one Malcolm, it's supposed to be for the chief local rep, but Francesca said he'd probably skip it as it's in English.'

'Thank you, Giles. I am quite indebted to UUP. You really have all been most helpful.'

'Cheers,' said Luciana, looking up at the statue, 'Bloody hell. If they put that loincloth any lower we could tell whether he was circumcised or not.'

Giles coughed, 'Actually, as he was Jewish, we'd have to assume he was.'

'Yeah. The unkindest cut. I was joking. It's a bit homoerotic and in your face for a lecture hall. Too gory.'

'One assumes that as it's a seminary, most lectures would be on a religious topic,' said Giles.

'It doesn't suit ELT talks on *Fun Classroom Games For Primary Schools,* though. I find it creepy,' she turned to Malcolm O'Reilly, 'That's my talk tomorrow. In a side room, not in here, thank Chri...,' she paused to look at the statue, '... goodness.'

Gloria pointed at the nearest Roman soldier, 'They haven't updated the Italian army uniforms for a few years,' she said, and cackled.

Mavis frowned, 'They're just dressed up like that to get money from foolish tourists,' she said. Each Roman soldier was standing with a seedy-looking photographer. Most were smoking.

'Nicely turned legs,' said Gloria, 'Very muscular and a good tan too. Short skirt. It must be very draughty round the dangly bits.'

The nearest one noticed their interest and walked over. The breast plate was dented gold tin. The under-tunic was shiny red nylon. The 'leather 'flaps were beige plastic. The helmet was a couple of sizes too big for him. There was an anchor tattoo on his forearm. Mavis recoiled as his cigarette smoke engulfed them.

'Hey, ladies … you wanna picture of you in front-a the Colosseum? Souvenir. Me and you together?'

'Does he actually have any film in that camera?' said Mavis.

'You pay when-a you collect - over there. One hour only. Two pictures? Or just-a one for yours house?'

'He thinks we're a pair of dykes,' said Gloria, then noticing Mavis's open mouthed shock, 'You know, I'll be Glad if you'll be Frank.'

'Decadence!' said Mavis, 'Depravity! Perversion! This is just what The Reverend told us! Filth! Get away from us!'

The Roman soldier shrugged, 'Fuck you!' he muttered.

'Only in your dreams,' said Gloria, and scampered after the departing Mavis.

The stern and tiny elderly lady who was introducing the speaker spoke in a dead flat monotone. The microphone was pointing at her forehead. Malcolm O'Reilly struggled to understand her.

'Is she speaking in Italian?' he whispered to Luciana.

She giggled, 'Good one.'

'It's a genuine question,' he protested.

'No, English. It just sounds Italian. As a matter of fact, she's American. Maria Gandolfini. Been here donkeys' years. President of the teachers' association. You get used to it. She's talking about the importance of the communicative approach in syllabus design. That's Ubaldini's topic.'

'She's not a communicator, is she?'

'No.'

Malcolm looked around. He'd been expecting to be shushed for whispering, but it seemed pretty widespread.

Ubaldini stood from a high backed oak chair at the rear of the stage and walked to the podium. He inclined his head in tribute to the polite applause, then raised one hand, and it stopped. He walked forward, put a sheaf of papers on the lectern and extracted gold reading glasses from his pocket. He solemnly placed them on his prominent nose and adjusted them slowly and carefully. He began to read aloud, also in a monotone and that Italian final vowel sound seemed to be on every word. He had his head down, looking down. He was not working from notes, but he was reading a complete text of the lecture.

'Fuck me, he's worse!' hissed Luciana.

Malcolm O'Reilly picked up that the aim of language education was communication, and that the syllabus enshrined in the Council of Europe Threshold Level would revolutionize textbooks. He looked around the room. Everyone was listening in dutiful silence. He began to struggle to stay awake.

Luciana and Giles walked back to the book exhibition with him. O'Reilly tried to remember whether anything of significance had been said, but it was as if all memory of the last fifty minutes had been totally eradicated.

'It was like watching paint dry,' said Luciana, 'I've never been that bored in years.'

Giles nodded, 'Depending on the shade of paint. Beige or magnolia perhaps. Watching a brighter hue drying would have been considerably more interesting.'

'Unbelievable,' said O'Reilly, 'It's as if changing the syllabus shape but continuing to read aloud in a boring monotone improves language teaching. As I've always said, teacher skills and enthusiasm are vastly more important than the label put on the language.'

Giles nodded, 'I do wish someone could impart that to Graham Donaldson.'

O'Reilly smiled, 'I have been attempting to do so for many years, Giles. However, he never pays attention. Perhaps the greatest teacher skill is demonstrating enormous interest in what the student, or indeed the Director of Studies, is saying.'

Francesca had spent the plenary sitting with Graham Donaldson. He seemed quite incapable of operating independently. Even the task of finding his way from the book exhibition to the plenary hall alone was beyond him. He'd had to ask Francesca to show him the way and walk with him. He also fidgeted throughout the talk. As it finished, she stood, 'What did you think of it?'

'Utter nonsense,' said Graham, 'Claptrap. Burble. Bunkum ...' another list was coming to mind, 'Rubbish. Blather. Humbug. Balderdash and Tommyrot.'

'So no positives then?'

'Absolutely none. The fellow hasn't a clue as to what he's talking about.'

'Oh, dear,' she said, 'That might be a problem. I've had to invite

Ubaldini to dinner with us this evening. It wasn't my idea. It was a direct instruction from head office. I'm so sorry.'

———

There was a litre carafe between two. The wine was thin and sharp, but at least plentiful. Gloria compared the 'Genuine Roman Lunch' with the feast she had enjoyed with Malkie the night before. This was simply fusilli with tomato sauce sprinkled with Parmesan dust. She'd had better in England. Still, the coach load of American tourists at the long tables were hoovering it up.

'No meat,' complained Mavis, 'You'd think there'd be pepperoni or salami. Or a Bolognese sauce.'

'Some of us are Jewish,' said the woman next to her, 'If it's vegetarian at least it's kosher.'

'So where you from, hon?' asked Mavis.

'Brooklyn,' said the woman, 'And we get better Italian-American food there than this. You call this Parmesan? It's just a speckle.'

'Not much of a lunch,' said Mavis peevishly.

'You ever had deep fried mozzarella?' asked the woman, 'There's a place on Long Island that does a block of it near a foot long.'

'You sure you don't want any?' said Gloria as she refilled her own glass to the brim.

'Teetotal,' said Mavis, 'Temperance congregation. You'd think they'd have Coca Cola.' Mavis stared glumly at the glass of sparkling water, 'Or even Pepsi.'

'All the more wine for me,' said Gloria. She took a swig, puckered her lips and examined the glass, 'It's not too bad once you get used to it.'

———

Luciana walked back with Malcolm O'Reilly to the book exhibition hall. It had filled up already with teachers coming from the plenary.

She paused at the Eden and Churchill stand. A woman's ample bottom was sticking through the garish E & C table-cloth.

'Elizabeth?' said Luciana.

The bottom wriggled backwards and a woman in a floral print frock stood up, 'Oh, Luciana. Hello.'

'This is Malcolm O'Reilly from World English Centre, the language school.'

'How do you do,' said Elizabeth and extended her hand.

'How do you do,' said O'Reilly.

'Bit of a bother,' said Elizabeth, 'I nipped along to get a coffee after the plenary, and I got chatting, as one does, and I've only just got back,' she seemed tearful, 'And all the cassettes and teachers' books for Ryan Babbit's new textbook have gone. The lot! It's the first day. I had to carry thirty teacher's books from London with me, excess baggage. Not one left. Not even a copy for poor Ryan to use in his talk. He's such a nice chap, by the way. Terribly good company. I know he didn't bring one, expecting to collect a copy here. There'll be fireworks when Head Office finds out. So sorry. Am I gabbling on? It's alright for you, Luciana. You've got the bods from the local office to keep an eye on things if you want to powder your nose. I'm on my own here.'

'You left the cassettes in the cases, and put all the teachers' books on the table?' said Luciana incredulously, 'They'll all have gone. They'll see them as free samples. Or that's what they'll say if you catch the bastards.'

'None went in Copenhagen last weekend,' wailed Elizabeth.

'The book store at the end of the exhibition hall will have at least one copy,' said Luciana, 'Though you may have to buy it.'

'What about the other books?' said Elizabeth, 'Oh, no! The dictionaries have gone too!' She pointed at an empty display stand, 'And the cassettes for the other courses. How am I going to get to the book store without them lifting all the other books too?'

Malcolm O'Reilly patted her hand, 'Now, Elizabeth. My table's just over there. I'm sure I can wait between the two while you go and fetch a book.'

Francesca had finally got the detailed programme and was fuming, 'I can't believe they did this!'

Luciana nodded, 'Utter bastards.'

Giles and Graham exchanged glances. 'What's the problem?' asked Giles.

'Look at five o'clock,' said Francesca, 'This is the most important time. The beginning of the evening session.'

Giles took the programme, 'I see. Ubaldini is in the plenary hall again.'

'He is talking on his new Business English course. It is for Dante … a publisher from Torino … Turin. It is commercial. All the five o'clock sessions are commercial. Graham is here in the Ignatius Loyola Room … just one hundred seats.'

'Considerably smaller,' said Giles.

'But then look … the other two main authors from British publishers are speaking at exactly the same time. Raymond O'Leary from Truman Education in the Thomás de Torquemada Room, you know, the *Passport* author. Then Ryan Babbit from Eden and Churchill in the Francisco Pizzaro Room. O'Leary and Babbit are the two most famous speakers at this conference. All three are at the same time in one hundred seat rooms, so in competition for seats. While Ubaldini is in the two thousand seat room!'

Giles pondered, 'At least they've rated Graham along with them. The names are all Spanish,' he mused.

Graham shook his head, 'O'Leary's an Irish name. Babbit isn't Spanish.'

'No, no. The rooms. Loyola, Torquemada, Pizzaro … they're all Spanish.'

'This was called the Spanish Seminary,' said Francesca.

'Wasn't Torquemada the Grand Inquisitor?' said Giles, 'Then Loyola founded the Jesuits and Pizzaro conquered the Incas. Not a pleasant lot, all in all. Still, I suppose I'm not a militant sixteenth century Spanish Catholic.'

'Roman Catholic,' corrected Graham.

'A Spanish Roman Catholic,' said Giles, 'Can you do anything about it, Francesca?'

'I will speak to Truman and to Eden and Churchill. We must object together. But it will be too late for today.'

'That's why the crafty sods kept the detailed programme back until today,' added Luciana, 'We kept asking while we were setting up the stand last night, so the local office could make up signs with speaking times and rooms on. They just said they hadn't assigned the rooms.'

Five minutes to five. The three rooms were in a row off the mahogany-panelled lobby which was lined with gloomy biblical paintings in ornate gilt frames. Martyrdom in a variety of excruciatingly painful ways was the prevailing theme. Whipping. Stoning. Burning. Drowning. Castration. Spikes under fingernails. Stretching on the rack. Eviscerating. Extracting teeth. Arrows. Beheading. Savaged by lions. Upside down crucifixion.

A crowd was pushing and shoving outside of each of the three doors. Francesca took Graham's arm at the Ignatius Loyola room, '*Andiamo*, come with me, Graham. I will get you to the front.'

The room was jam packed. People were standing all around the walls. The centre gangway was full of people sitting on the floor. The front area was packed with even more sitting on the floor. They were sitting on the stage. Francesca elbowed, kicked, pushed and squeezed through to the microphone, pulling a trembling Graham with her. There was just room for Graham to stand, though he would not be able to move. The air was thick and fetid. Graham loosened his tie and undid his top shirt button. The sweat was already soaking through.

Giles and Luciana had not followed Francesca to the front. 'Bugger. It's like the Tower Ballrooms ladies' bog in Blackpool on a Saturday night. Worse even,' said Luciana.

'More like the Black Hole of Calcutta,' said Giles, 'Let's check the other rooms.'

O'Leary and Babbit's rooms were equally crowded. Giles followed Luciana to the door of the huge plenary hall. There was Ubaldini at the lectern, with an extensive book display either side of him. A banner with 'Dante Torino' was hung along the front of the stage. Around thirty people were sitting there in the front couple of rows, listening to his drone as he read aloud.

Giles looked at the book display, 'It's called *Mind Your Business*. Do you think they understand the meaning?'

'And the fucker's doing it in Italian,' said Luciana, 'It's supposed to be an English Language conference.'

Luciana found Francesca in the hotel bar.

'Ah, Luciana. A *digestivo*? Cynar? I need something. The day has been stress, stress and stress.'

'Stressful,' said Luciana. Whoops, she thought. Correcting Francesca always resulted in a cool look. 'Cynar? Is that the one that tastes disgusting?'

'Artichokes liquor.'

'Is it? Bugger. I'll have a Bloody Mary then.'

Francesca beckoned the waiter over.

'Yes, ma'am?' he said.

Francesca ordered, 'You see he naturally assumed that I was English.'

Luciana knew it was a riposte for the 'stressful' correction. 'I was wondering,' she said, 'Can we invite Mr and Mrs O'Reilly to dinner? It's a big party anyway, and they're on their own.'

Francesca considered, 'Yes. We must consider that he is the Director of Studies of one of the largest schools in England. Please do. Also a very nice gentleman. And remind me to call Patrick O'Toole in the UK. I shall ask to put the costs of their meal on the UUP Britain entertainment account.'

They assembled in the hotel lobby at eight o'clock. Francesca and Luciana represented UUP Italia on their own. The local office had firmly declined to come out on a Saturday night after working all day on the stand, citing family obligations. 'This would never happen in Naples or Florence,' said Francesca, shaking her head, 'It is not hospitable. I have told you. Rome is different.'

Giles and Graham stood uncomfortably together. Malcolm and Gloria O'Reilly were sitting. Gloria was still a little unsteady after the whole litre of red wine to herself for lunch. Fortunately the two hours snoring in the hotel room had revived her sufficiently.

'Ubaldini will be late,' Francesca said, 'He will wish to make an entrance,' she looked round carefully, 'There was quite a fuss with the committee. Fortunately it did not involve us, though we must agree with Eden & Churchill and make a complaint. Ryan Babbit was incand ...' she faltered.

'Incandescent?' said Giles helpfully.

'Exactly. It was about the rooms being too small, and the speakers from the three largest British publishers being on at the same time as one another. So Ryan Babbit confronted Signora Gandolfini. Or possibly affronted Signora Gandolfini,' Francesca preened at her own language command, 'They were angry when he accused them of a sewing up.'

Luciana coughed, 'Stitch-up,' she murmured.

'He then complained that all his books and cassettes had been stolen from the Eden and Churchill stand. Of course, they said it is not their business. Then it got bad,' she paused dramatically, 'For Ryan Babbit declared the conference participants were a pack of thieves. This offended them greatly,' she considered, 'Perhaps because it is true. So they said he would never be invited to a conference from their association again. And he replied ...'

'Fuck you?' suggested Luciana, 'No. Go fuck yourselves.'

'Precisely. The latter. How did you know?'

'I'm psychic. No, not really, but it's what I'd've said.'

Francesca smiled, 'In fact offending Gandolfini is not important. She only promotes American authors. Ubaldini only promotes Italian ones. Their disapproval is irrelevant. After all, Babbit's book is the market leader currently.'

'I've taught it. It's the best,' put in Luciana, then noting Graham's expression, 'Present company excepted. I haven't taught yours, Graham. I'm sure it's, er, very good. Um, just as good.'

Graham glowered. He'd seen Babbit's book in Bournemouth. It had functional chapter headings, and flashy cartoon strips. It was not at all his sort of thing.

'He's a brilliant speaker too,' said Luciana, 'I saw him in Bologna. He had everyone singing along ... there are songs in the book.'

Graham shuddered at the thought.

Ubaldini arrived at a quarter past eight. He had an immaculate camel coloured overcoat, a silk scarf and a trilby hat. Francesca conducted the introductions. Malcolm O'Reilly noted that he and Ubaldini were easily the smartest men there. You would think Graham could have made the effort to at least change after the day. There was a sour odour of armpits about him. Giles was a pleasant fellow, but the grey suit, white shirt and college tie were formal, but not in the least attractive. Francesca was beautifully attired at least. Lovely pearls. Luciana had changed into a short skirt over black leggings, set off by a Ramones T-shirt with a neck chain which carried three real heavy Mercedes bonnet badges. Gloria, well, he was afraid to say that the expression 'mutton dressed as lamb' would come to mind, much as he loved her. The skirt was too short. The neckline too low. The lipstick too bright.

They set off to the restaurant. Luciana had noted Gloria's difficulties stumbling along with her high heels on the cobbles and linked arms with her to lead the way. They were chatting merrily. Giles was walking with Francesca, with Graham trailing behind. Malcolm O'Reilly found himself in step with Ubaldini.

'I must say, Dottore Ubaldini, that I find Italy most impressive. Such well-dressed men and women. If only the British took so much trouble in sartorial matters.'

They both stared at Graham, trudging along sullenly just in front of them.

'Thank you, Dottore O'Reilly,' he said, 'I note that you are the British exception.'

'Please, do call me Malcolm. I do not hold a doctorate. I am a plain mister. My own education was interrupted by the war, and my language education came during my extensive travels.'

Ubaldini looked puzzled, 'You are Dottore Donaldson's director, are you not?'

'I am, but Donaldson is not a doctor either. Cert.Ed ... that is, certificate of education, I believe.'

Unbaldini smiled wolfishly, 'He is not a doctor? A great surprise. In this case, I think we may move to first name terms. I am Sirio.'

'Thank you so much, Sirio,' said Malcolm O'Reilly. Again his own communication abilities were at the fore. Everyone had told him what a stiff and frosty fellow Ubaldini was.

Francesca considered a seating plan. In an ideal world, she'd have placed herself at the head of the table, then Giles Winthrop and Malcolm O'Reilly at either side of her. Luciana and Gloria would be next, opposite each other with Ubaldini and Graham Donaldson at the end furthest away from her. It couldn't be. Both were serial moaners to higher authority. She would have to be sandwiched between Ubaldini and Donaldson, then Luciana and Gloria next. Luciana, as an Italian speaker would have to put up with being next to Ubaldini. Then Malcolm and Giles would be opposite each other at the end. She glued a smile to her face. 'Dottore Ubaldini, please, would you care to sit next to me?'

'*Grazie.*'

'*Prego.*'

Malcolm O'Reilly watched the waiter. He went straight to Francesca, and handed her the large leather bound wine list. Giles said 'I've noticed this all week. The waiters go straight to Francesca.'

'She is sitting at the head of the table.'

'I know,' said Giles, 'That position also maintains the male / female alternate placing. But in most countries, the waiter would look for the senior male, and probably go to Ubaldini. Here it's the senior woman. I've noticed it at other tables, and asked Francesca about it. Women tend to order the food. You'll see the bill will go to her at the end.'

'She has a certain air of authority about her.'

'She certainly has,' said Giles. Wistfully, thought Malcolm. The man was obviously public school. He probably had a crush on a stern matron.

'Tell me about yourself,' said Malcolm. 'Where are you from?'

'I grew up in Cambridge, but I was a school near Bournemouth, as it happens.'

'Canford?' suggested Malcolm, 'We've been negotiating to run summer holiday courses on their premises.'

'Exactly, so as I lived in Cambridge, of course I went to Oxford. A strict old-fashioned education is ideal for editing.'

'I can see that,' said Malcolm.

Francesca called to them, 'May I suggest the *Risotto alla Romana* to begin? It is typical.'

'What's in it?' asked Graham peevishly.

'It has meat. Liver and *animelle*. I don't know the English word. With Marsala and pecorino, which is cheese from sheep.'

'Ugh. Disgusting,' said Luciana, '*Animelle* means testicles!'

'No, no. This is a common mistake,' said Francesca. 'They are from the calf, but from the pancreas and here ...' she touched her throat.

'Thyroid?' suggested Luciana.

'The English are always fussing over what they will eat,' said Ubaldini, 'In Italy we eat everything.'

'Yeah. Songbirds,' said Luciana, 'Also disgusting.'

Malcolm O'Reilly was leafing through his little phrase book. Restaurants. Menus. Food. Meat. There it was. 'Sweetbreads!' he exclaimed, 'They're called sweetbreads.'

'Sweet bread? I think this is a mistake,' said Ubaldini.

'No, that's the English word,' said Luciana, 'It's offal. I've heard of it. That's why I thought it was testicles.'

'I can assure you not,' said Francesca.

'It is not bread. I am certain,' insisted Ubaldini.

'Is there anything else?' asked Gloria.

'There is spaghetti with a simple sauce of pecorino and olive oil,' said Francesca.

'I'll have that,' said Gloria.

'Me too,' added Luciana.

'I should prefer that,' said Graham.

'When in Rome ...' said Giles. 'I'll try the risotto.'

'Why not?' said Malcolm, 'Yes, risotto for me.'

The waiter came over. 'OK, you guys. What you having for starters? The *risotto alla Romana* is ours house speciality. Maybe not for most British though. I don't want y'all puking up when I say what's in it. We had a couple of Yanks last week what turned purple when I told them. But it's not bollocks, I'll tell you that. I mean, it's not bull balls, not that it's not rubbish.' He laughed. 'So, ladies first. What's for you ma'am?' he wrote it down, 'And for you sweetheart?' he indicated Luciana, then Gloria, 'What about you, hon?' He laughed at their order, 'I see she don't like *animelle,* and she don't not like it neither.'

The main course order went much the same way, *with saltimbocca alla Romana* being the dish of the day. The waiter retreated. Ubaldini stared after him. 'This is typical. These ignorant common people. They are thinking they speak the English. But all is bad. This *cameriere* said "she don't" and then the double negative,' he shuddered.

'Triple negative actually,' suggested Giles, 'She don't not like it neither.'

Graham perked up, 'Hmm, if the second negative, er, negates or reverses the first negative, what is the effect of a third negative? Would it reverse it back again? Or not?'

'We are in Italy! Why does the *cameriere* not speak in Italian?'

'We were conversing in English,' said Francesca gently, 'He naturally assumed we were English.'

Luciana shook her head. Given Ubaldini's heavy Italian accent the assumption seemed unlikely to her.

'Also these are ignorant Americanisms. These people collect some words from some American *turista* and then they repeat these errors loud and rude,' said Ubaldini.

'Tourists,' said Luciana, 'loudly and rudely.'

Malcolm O'Reilly coughed, 'In fact these are not Americanisms at all. Except perhaps "you guys." Double negation is simply meant to be emphatic. This is language, it is not mathematics. Don't + not equals do. That's nonsense. You will find double negation is widespread. Also, the use of "he don't" like the use of "I were" or "We was" is present in many British regions.'

'I were about to say that,' said Luciana, 'Definitely I were.'.

'At my grammar school there was a teacher, a Mr Cutler, who used to say "Was you talking, boy? Was you?" I will admit that he taught only woodwork. We are not hyper-critical of such regional uses, as long as we understand them,' continued Malcolm, 'Which flexibility is why English has become a *lingua franca*.'

'In Italian, we are seeking perfection in grammar. We look downwards on those with poor grammar,' said Ubaldini.

'Look down, not downwards,' muttered Luciana. Francesca glanced at her and put a finger to her lips.

'In fact,' said Malcolm, 'The waiter spoke well. He was fluent, colloquial and confident and had a good accent.'

'American accent!' said Ubaldini.

'That is not a problem,' said Malcolm, 'There's absolutely nothing wrong with American accents, nor Americanisms. It's all English. I was particularly impressed by his accent. He lacked that Italian intrusive final vowel sound.'

'What final vowel sound?' said Ubaldini.

Malcolm couldn't resist, 'Well, you said "What-a final-a- vowel-a sound-a" so one might say his accent was better than yours. Not that yours is unclear of course. '

The silence was deafening. Ubaldini was red in the face. 'I am the head of the linguistics department at the university in Bologna. It was a university in 1088. An older university than your Oxford or

Cambridge. While you ...' he turned and indicated Graham, 'And also you, are not qualified!'

'My sincere apologies,' said Malcolm with a smile, 'No offence was intended.'

'He always says that when he's been bloody rude,' Gloria said to Luciana.

Graham had been thinking about it, 'O'Reilly's quite right for once,' he said, 'Both on the subject of double negatives, and on regionalisms. Yes, and on pronunciation too. I suppose there are some things non-native speakers never pick up. For example, we would say "speak English" rather than "speak the English."'

Giles came in, 'There isn't a great deal in it you know. Bologna and Oxford. There is some evidence that teaching began in Oxford as early as 1096. Cambridge is rather later, I agree. I believe Paris was actually third in 1200, followed by Cambridge in 1231. Then Oxford and Cambridge spawned American universities like Harvard, which is in Cambridge, Massachusetts ...' he trailed off. Perhaps it was inappropriate. Perhaps it was showing off, something he had learned to avoid as the brightest boy in his class at school.

Francesca waited. No one spoke, 'So, Mrs O'Reilly,' she said brightly, 'Please tell us about your tour of Rome.'

Ubaldini sniffed the wine, 'This is local.'

'Yes,' said Francesca, 'The waiter recommended the house wine. It is a local one which they get directly from the grower. Is there a problem?'

'There is some excellent Barolo on the wine listing, I believe. I can see the bottles over there. Next to the Chianti Classico,' Ubaldini swilled the wine round in his glass, 'This is not the quality I would serve to guests.'

'I thought our British guests might enjoy a local wine,' said Francesca.

Gloria drained her glass, 'It's a lot better than the crap we got at lunchtime.' She reached for the bottle and refilled her glass.

'Lazio is not renowned for red wine,' said Ubaldini, 'I would expect UUP to afford more.'

'Never look a gift horse in the mouth,' said Luciana cheerfully.

'It's most enjoyable,' said Malcolm, and he took a sip.

'Yes, yes, I like it too,' said Graham, for once prepared to run with the crowd, 'To have afforded more, by the way.'

'What?' snapped Ubaldini.

'As the wine is already on the table, "to have afforded" rather than "to afford." I will admit that I am being somewhat picky.' Graham felt a little buzz of pleasure when both Winthrop and O'Reilly laughed.

'What do English people know of wine?' said Ubaldini.

'You'll find the Oxford colleges know a good claret at high table when they see one,' said Giles, 'Though perhaps you're unfamiliar with French wine.'

'England is a country that is serving warm beer,' said Ubaldini.

'Real ale should be served at room temperature,' said Giles, 'I thought everybody knew that.'

Francesca didn't know how to handle this. The complaints to Head Office were already certain, and as deeply objectionable as Ubaldini was, there was the thought that she should defend a fellow countryman against a united British attack.

At that point the waiter arrived. Malcolm O'Reilly turned and smiled at him, 'I must compliment you on your excellent English,' he said, 'We are all English teachers here and we were saying how well you speak. Where did you learn?'

'I don't not study,' said the waiter, 'I just only meeting the people. I speak. I like the people. I also had the American girlfriend. Is the most best way to learn.' He winked at O'Reilly, 'In the bed. I am chatty man.'

'Most best!' snorted Ubaldini. They all ignored him.

'Dead right,' said Gloria, 'My friend Cheryl went out with a toreador. Well, an ex-toreador. That's what he said. He was more into fire-eating and a bit of flamenco dancing by the time she met him. Batley Variety Club. She spoke Spanish like a native by the end of it.'

The waiter immediately topped up her glass.

'*Gracias,*' she said.

'That's Spanish,' said Malcolm O'Reilly wearily.

'Is it? Well, it's all the same.'

The line-up for the walk back had changed. Francesca felt she had to walk with Ubaldini in the circumstances. Malcolm walked with Luciana, and Giles with Gloria. Graham Donaldson remained the lone figure at the back.

'It's incumbent on a gentleman to walk on the outside,' Giles was explaining, 'This is why the British walk and drive on the left. It dates back to an era when footpads were a problem. The man on the outside had his right arm free to draw his sword, which was worn on his left hip, or by the nineteenth century, he had a sturdy walking stick in his right hand. His presence also protected her long skirts from the water and worse thrown up by passing horses and carts.'

'No wonder you get on with Malkie,' said Gloria, 'That's just the sort of stuff he spends his life telling people. Mind you, I never understood skirts brushing along the ground. Think of the filth you'd get on the hems. Stage skirts are always a couple of inches short. Like when me and Malkie did *Pygmalion* it was well above the ankles. I was Eliza Doolittle. I mean, dog shit wasn't the half of it in them days.'

'I assume Malcolm was Henry Higgins?' said Giles.

"How did you guess?'

'So what do you do if a student says "I were" or "He don't" in a lesson,' asked Luciana.

'Ah,' said Malcolm, 'Is it a fluency stage or an accuracy stage? In an oral drill or a written exam, you'd correct it. However, if a student was saying something meaningful, and doing so at some speed, you'd ignore it.'

'You try telling an Italian Director of Studies that,' said Luciana, 'That's why they're such reluctant speakers. Terrified of making mistakes.'

They both jumped at the loud blare of a car horn behind them on the narrow cobbled street. They'd assumed it was traffic free. They shrank back as a long white limousine swept past, making no attempt to avoid them. The wing mirror actually brushed Malcolm's arm hard, and as he moved back, Luciana was pushed into the rough stone wall.

Luciana had a finger raised in the air, 'You stupid fucking cunt!' she shouted, 'Jesus fucking Christ, you could have killed us!'

Francesca turned, 'Shhh! Didn't you see? Through the open window?'

'No, what?'

'It was His Holiness ... the *papa*, the pope in the back seat. He will have heard!' she said in horror.

Luciana shrugged, 'Still fucking dangerous driving.'

Gloria giggled, 'Still, there's one thing, Malkie. I reckon if the pope had run you over and it was his fault you'd go straight up to heaven.'

Ubaldini was bristling with anger, 'This is not amusing! It is sacrilege. Also, I have never heard such disgusted language even from the man, also never from the woman.!'

'Disgusting,' said Graham helpfully, 'Not disgusted. We'd say "a man" rather than "the man" and perhaps you were trying to say "let alone a woman."'

Luciana nudged Malcom, 'Was that a fluency stage or an accuracy stage?' Malcolm laughed.

'This is the typical British! You all drink too much!' said Ubaldini.

'Fuck off,' muttered Luciana, not quite quietly enough.

They stood there in silence.

'Well, I thought this evening went jolly well,' said Giles.

Ubaldini could not understand why they all started laughing.

There hadn't been one there the day before. Graham Donaldson was delighted to see it, peeping out from beneath the Italian, German and French newspapers on the side table in the breakfast restaurant. An English paper! Rather, a paper in English, the *International Herald-Tribune*. He grabbed the lone copy and hurried to a table. He sorely missed the *Daily Telegraph* with its crossword, but this would have to do. He rather hoped that being immersed in a newspaper would fend off his erstwhile companions from accosting him at breakfast too. As the others had repaired to the bar on their return to the hotel the previous evening, they might not be too early at breakfast. Graham had been so exhausted by so much company that he had gone straight to bed, only to wake up an hour later, completely alert. That state lasted several hours, so much so that he had amused himself with a mental list of animal characteristics applied to humans which could feature in a future textbook. Not the ridiculous similes favoured by older textbooks, like *as strong as an ox* or *as timid as a mouse* or *as blind as a bat*. There'd been far too much of that nonsense when Graham first started teaching. Rather a man might be an old dog. A woman might be a bitch or a silly cow, or if ill-tempered a vixen. Two women arguing might be a catfight. Two people might fight like cat and dog. A cunning fellow might be a fox who wanted a lion's share of available resources. Someone who persisted stubbornly with a point would be like a dog with a bone. Dog carts were not drawn by dogs. Then there was donkey jacket, and donkey engine. Where had those come from?

He started glancing through the newspaper. Far too much material of American interest only. Then a headline caught his eye:

MULES ARRESTED WITH HORSE

How strange. Such a typical newspaper ploy. He recalled the headline 'Welsh Wails' recently in an article on holiday homes taking available accommodation from locals. This story concerned two middle-aged people who were returning from a vacation in Acapulco. They had arrived at the airport in New York, only to be arrested when heroin was found in a parcel they were carrying. Heroin was known as 'horse' according to the article. Their story was that a very pleasant Mexican chap they met in a restaurant had asked them if they would mind delivering the parcel to his brother who lived near them in Brooklyn. He claimed it contained family mementos and photographs which were far too precious to risk losing in the mail. There were tears in his eyes as he described the only photos of his recently deceased mother. He had presented them with a bottle of a rare tequila for their trouble. A mule was a person inveigled into transporting contraband, then. The newspaper mentioned a British novel about heroin, *Horse Under Water,* not that Graham had heard of it.

Graham Donaldson took out his notebook. Mule was worth adding to his list, though he would avoid teaching 'horse.' He wondered how people could possibly be that stupid.

'There's Graham Donaldson,' whispered Gloria, 'I hope he hasn't seen us.'

'He's lost in his newspaper,' said Malcolm O'Reilly. He leafed through the copies on the table, 'Apparently it's the only English language one too.'

'I'm not sure I want to see an old ceiling,' said Gloria. 'Whoever painted it.'

'Well, it's the other tour, and it ends after lunch right by the conference,' said Malcolm, indicating the brochure on the table, 'St. Peter's, Vatican Museum and Sistine Chapel.'

'Luciana said I'd have to wear a headscarf,' said Gloria, 'And I haven't brought one. I mean why would I? No bare arms either, not that I was going to. Anyway, Francesca said I could borrow one from her. A scarf. They're such lovely girls.'

'Good morning.'

They both turned, 'Good morning, Giles,' said Malcolm, 'I trust you slept well.'

'Yes, thank you. Oh, dear. No English newspapers. Still, I'll take the French one, unless you were ...'

'No, no,' said Malcolm hurriedly, 'We're fine.'

'I've never seen you try to read a French newspaper,' said Gloria, 'When we were in France you always went and got the *Daily Mail*.'

———

Luciana refilled her cup, 'I wouldn't worry, Cesca. After all the bastard doesn't write for us. He's promoting his books from Dante. Fuck him.'

'He is influential on the committee and senior at Bologna university. I was told to be nice to him. Then you all acted as a gang against ...'

'Ganged up on him?' suggested Luciana, 'Hard to resist.'

'He'll complain.'

'Get in first. Point out he fucked up our promotion by shoving

Donaldson in a small room. Then he used the main hall to promote his Dante business book,' Luciana grinned, 'Then suggest that UUP drop his book. Out of date, not up to our high standards. Both are true. Yeah, put it out of print, delete the fucker from our list.'

'That's quite aggressive,' said Francesca.

'Best form of defence is attack,' said Luciana, 'You must have read Machiavelli.'

'I'm sure Machiavelli didn't say that. I think it's Sun Tzu *L'Arte Della Guerra*. NIE publish an edition.'

'*The Art of War*, OK, but I bet Machiavelli would have said it if he'd been asked,' concluded Luciana. 'So stick it to him.'

Francesca shrugged, 'I might. At least we have Graham's plenary in the main hall today.'

'Right after Ryan Babbit. I'm not sure that the comparison will help him.'

As requested by Francesca, Giles waited in the hotel lobby to escort Graham Donaldson the few hundred metres to the conference. It was the major talk of the tour. Giles thought Graham could have at least made an effort with his crumpled clothes. The hotel had a laundry and a one hour pressing service after all, which Giles had utilised.

They set out. As so often Giles found Graham's silence was forcing him to chatter, 'Still making notes for the next book, are we?'

'Sorry, Winthrop?' Graham wondered why people said 'are we' in preference to 'are you.' It was worth a note.

'I was wondering if you'd given more thought to asking WEC for an unpaid sabbatical so that you could finish it.'

'I am considering it,' said Graham. Considering escaping from that preening, overbearing, pompous fellow O'Reilly, he added mentally.

'We would need to assign considerable editorial and design

resources, you see, so we would be most grateful for an early response.'

'Would you indeed?'

'It seems an opportune time to ask, as Mr O'Reilly is in Rome with us.'

'Hardly with us. He's promoting the school.'

Giles thought it best to change the subject, 'So tell me about the latest set of notes.'

Graham brightened, 'Ah, yes. Animal and human comparison. I read a most interesting piece this morning. Do you know that a mule is someone persuaded to carry contraband?'

'I had heard it. There was a case last month at Heathrow. A young girl had been persuaded to swallow a, er, well, a condom with heroin inside it to go through customs. It burst in her stomach and killed her.'

'Good Lord!' Graham considered, 'How would they get it out?'

'I assume that it would emerge in the fullness of time via the normal channel,' said Giles. The thought came, or would they simply capture her and slit her stomach open? 'I believe people also conceal condoms with drugs in, um, their orifices. It's why customs officials might check suspects with rubber gloves.'

'Check the orifice?' said Graham in horror.

'Orifices,' said Giles, 'Women have two.'

'There's no need to be coarse,' said Graham curtly.

'More often they ask some unsuspecting person to carry a parcel for them.'

'As in the American example,' said Graham, 'Who would be that stupid?'

'Exactly. There was an example on a plane where people were asked to carry a bottle of duty free whisky through customs for other passengers who had more than their limit. Apparently, drugs were dissolved in the alcohol, if that's possible, or perhaps it was simply liquid drugs or even powder. If it were a dark green or brown bottle, who would know?'

'I suppose you're right,' said Graham. They had arrived at the conference hall, and put on their lanyards.

———

They paused at the World English Centre stand. Malcolm O'Reilly was talking to Gabriella.

'Ah, Graham!' he said, 'I was hoping to find you. Here's Gabriella.'

Graham looked puzzled.

'Good morning, Mr Donaldson,' she said, 'It is so nice to see you here in my country. I look forward so much to your talk today. I was trying to get in yesterday, but there were too many people.'

Malcolm recognized Graham's look of total incomprehension, 'Barry Grant,' he emphasized the name, 'Will be so pleased to know that Gabriella found you here, won't he? You'll be able to tell him when you get back to the Intermediate staffroom.' Surely that should jog his memory.

'Ah, yes. Grant. Mm. Grant.'

'How long were you in Mr Donaldson's class, Gabriella?' Malcolm tried again.

'For three months. I remember your grammar classes so well.'

'Mmm. Yes. Italian, aren't you? I remember,' Graham lied.

Malcolm kept his eyes on the table. Italian? Not a hard guess, 'Gabriella kindly brought me a bottle of very special olive oil. From Bologna where she lives now,' he added, 'Gloria was thrilled .'

'The oil is from Emilia-Romagna province, not from the city,' she said.

'Of course. I meant you brought it with you. On the train. From Bologna.'

Graham's mouth was slightly open. His brows were furrowed. These people apparently presented olive oil to all and sundry. He'd spent a week transporting the stuff the length and breadth of the country. Why length and breadth? Why not length and width? Then you might say 'it's as broad as it's long.' Why not, 'as wide as it's long'? He'd better make a note.

Malcolm O'Reilly had to keep trying, 'As I recall, Gabriella, you were with us five years ago, in 1972. Barry Grant taught your class, as well as poor John Smith, until John Smith was hospitalized, that is.'

'And Mr Grace-Pitleigh taught us,' said Gabriella, 'You have an excellent memory.'

Graham looked irritated. Grace-Pitleigh? The man was an utter cad. Awful fellow. Constantly leering at female students. Smith was a noisy Yorkshireman. Always bellowing some piece of useless information in the staff room. Grinning all the time. Hospitalized? He remembered that Smith had departed suddenly. He had no recall of what had been wrong with the man. And so how was he expected to remember individual students?

Giles had picked up the situation, 'I'm so pleased to meet you, Gabriella. I'm Graham's editor. So you were one of his students?'

'I am now studying linguistics,' she said, 'With Dottore Ubaldini.'

'Really? What a marvellous compliment to your teaching, Graham. If you'd care to accompany us to the UUP stand, Gabriella, I'm sure Graham will be delighted to autograph a copy of *Intercourse* for you,' he picked up her worried look. She probably thought she'd have to buy it, 'With the compliments of UUP, of course.'

Mavis was patting the seat next to her, 'Gloria!' she called, 'Gloria! Over here! I knew you'd be on the tour! I saved you a seat, hon.'

Gloria looked round the tour minibus. There was no choice, but she had to wonder why Mavis, so upset by her remarks the day before, should seek her company. Then it struck her that Mavis simply craved company, any company, and the other Americans from her cruise ship had had enough and were avoiding her.

'Morning, Mavis,' Gloria took the seat, finding herself perched right on the edge as Mavis's ample bottom was occupying two thirds of it, 'I didn't think St Peter's and the Vatican would be your sort of thing.'

'Know thy enemy,' said Mavis.

Gloria dabbed her eyes, 'Malkie was right. It's beautiful. So sad. The way she's holding him, and looking down. I've welled right up!' She sniffed snottily.

Mavis stood next to her staring at *La Pietà*, 'Thou shalt not make unto thee any graven image or any likeness of any thing that is in heaven above, or that is in the Earth beneath, or that is in the water under earth. Thou shalt not bow down thyself to them, nor serve them. For I, the Lord thy God am a jealous God, visiting the iniquity of the fathers upon the children unto the third or fourth generation. Exodus.'

'That's a bit harsh,' said Gloria, 'Unto the third or fourth generation? Cruel, I call that. I mean look at it, it drips a mother's love. It's gorgeous.'

'Idolatry. The golden calf.'

'It's by Michelangelo. Malkie was telling me all about it. It's closed here this afternoon, too. He so wanted to see it.'

Mavis looked round the basilica carefully, then bent in and whispered, 'He liked other men.'

'Who? Malkie?'

'Michelangelo.'

'Did he? Live and let live, that's what I say. We've got plenty of good friends that way inclined. You do. In the theatre. It's normal.'

'It's not normal in Kansas!'

'Oh, I expect it is,' said Gloria, 'It's the same everywhere, you know. They just don't go round telling everyone about it.'

'Babylon!' Mavis looked up, 'We have white walls and plain glass windows in our church. So that we can look out through them and appreciate the glory of what God has created.'

'Mmm,' said Gloria, 'Depends what's outside. Malkie always wanted to produce *The Crucible*. That's about Puritans. We've seen it twice. He's very fond of Arthur Miller. We did *A View From The Bridge* last week at the school. Malkie was Eddie ... you know, the one who wants to fuc... screw his niece. It's a bit of an Arthur Miller theme. *The Crucible* too, though that's a housemaid, not his niece. Well, he was married to Marilyn Monroe. That'd have anyone thinking about sex all the time.' Gloria smiled to herself. That had had the desired effect of rooting Mavis to the spot in shock.

'We're in a church!' hissed Mavis.

'It was you who was going on about idolatry, and that the Pope was the anti-Christ,' said Gloria, 'So what's next? The ceiling, I reckon.'

Luciana put a cup of coffee from the tray on the table, 'There you are, Malcolm. Cesca sent me to get four cups, so I got you one too.'

'How very kind,' he said.

'Well, if she's got me skivvying around and doing the coffee, I can only hope it's a road to better things. How's it been going?'

'I've just given out my last brochure, apart from the display ones,' Malcolm O'Reilly held up an expanding wallet, 'It's been truly excellent. Best of all a chap from a college in Palermo just booked thirty student places for a month on condition we gave him a free teacher's course, plus in-family accommodation for himself and his wife,' he chuckled, 'He's arranging the air tickets for the group through his brother-in-law's travel agency so I'm sure he'll be doubly rewarded. My management in Switzerland is bound to agree. Nice chap. He came back ten minutes later with a bottle of grappa from his home village,' he rummaged under the counter and produced an unlabelled bottle, 'Straight from the barrel.'

'Excellent. You'll be able to watch a couple of talks then,' she said.

'I think I might. I'd rather like to hear Ryan Babbit. He starts in fifteen minutes. I've heard good things about him.'

'He's just over there, talking to Elizabeth,' she said, 'On the Eden & Churchill stand. Come on, she'll introduce you.'

Malcolm looked across the aisle. A tall man with jet black hair in an elaborate James Dean quiff... dyed, obviously ... was chatting to Elizabeth. He was wearing a pale green lightweight suit with an emerald green cravat.

Elizabeth beckoned him over, 'Ryan, you must meet Malcolm O'Reilly. He's Director of Studies of World English College.'

'World English Centre,' murmured Malcolm.

'Centre, of course!' said Elizabeth, 'Whoops! Egg on face here. I'll forget my own name next.'

'I'm sure you won't, Margaret,' said Luciana, 'You don't still think it's Elizabeth, do you?'

Ryan Babbit looked him up and down carefully. O'Reilly noticed he was checking out his immaculate polished shoes. His own were equally shiny, 'Bournemouth, eh? Aren't you the biggest school?'

'We are. You're in London, I believe?'

'North-East Polytechnic. You must know Bernard 'Benedict' Arnold from Euro-Lang.'

O'Reilly laughed, 'Do you call him that too? I must admit I'm unable to resist.'

'I've met him during my Dip. App. Ling lectures. I pop down to Portsmouth every so often to deliver my expertise. Isn't Graham Donaldson one of your people?'

'He is.'

Ryan Babbit looked at him quizzically, 'Odd. I'd never heard of him, and then he comes out with a major textbook for UUP with all their massive promotion, paid for by their alleged charitable status. I thought I knew absolutely everyone who was anyone. Yet there are these dark horses hiding away down in Bournemouth, beavering away. How the fuck did he name the book *Intercourse*?'

'A question I ask myself frequently.'

'Is it subversively ironic or simply naïve?'

'Complete lack of any awareness,' said Malcolm.

'How disappointing. I'm brimming with vulgar curiosity. I may watch his talk. You must introduce me to him at the reception this evening.'

'Which reception is that?' asked Malcolm.

'There's a reception for presenters, publishers and travelling promoters,' said Elizabeth, 'Haven't you had an invitation?'

'I'm afraid not.'

'I'll pick you up a couple,' said Luciana, 'None of the Rome office will want to go on a Sunday evening. You can have their cards. It's supposed to be shitty, but we'll go on to a proper dinner after. We have to go. It's held by Maria Gandolfini at the hotel next to her apartment. Basically, you've paid for a table. You deserve a glass of prosecco and a couple of crisps.'

'If your local Rome chappies decide to attend after all, I've got two spare,' said Elizabeth, 'They gave us four, and it's only me and Ryan. What with me being a one woman band, so to speak. I do envy you, Luciana.'

'At least you don't have to go and get coffee for a load of idle blokes,' said Luciana, and paused, 'Bugger. It'll be stone cold now. Never mind. I couldn't give a shit. I was thinking of spitting in it anyway'

'The reception will be a total bore,' said Ryan, 'I'm only going along to be cussed, because the Italian contingent really won't want me there. I may well create a scene,' he finished theatrically.

'I did hear about the altercation,' said Malcolm.

'Graham Donaldson must be equally angry.'

'I rather think not,' said Malcolm, 'It all seems to pass him by.'

'I know it's directly before your talk,' said Giles, 'But you should go and see Babbit. He's direct competition to your book after all. I would be remiss not to attend myself.'

'I'm not particularly interested,' said Graham, 'I have glanced briefly at the book.'

Francesca interrupted, 'You see, Graham, at these sort of events, people like it if you mention other speakers in a nice way. You could find just something you agree with and mention it in your talk.'

'I see that my time is not my own,' said Graham stiffly.

'You're perfectly free after the talk,' she said, 'Or you could do a little sightseeing around the Vatican.'

'On my own!' said Graham in horror, 'No, no. I suppose I shall have to attend.'

They found seats right at one side. Ryan Babbit was already standing at the lectern. Signora Gandolfini started to hobble on theatrically to introduce him. He held up his hand, 'Thank you, *Dottore*, but I prefer to use the whole time. No introduction, please. I can introduce myself.'

She gasped and retreated.

'Powerful move,' whispered Francesca, 'He also knows everyone knows who he is.'

Luciana pointed, 'Elizabeth was telling me. Eden and Churchill hired in their own sound system. Look at the speakers.' They were very large, with an open reel tape recorder on the table next to them. 'It cost a fortune, she said. They rented them in Rome.'

The first twenty minutes were pretty anodyne. Well-presented, but nothing was startlingly new. The overhead projector slides were professionally designed and printed in colour. Then he introduced the song, and explained it was from the textbook, one song for each unit. This was from 'Talking about the recent past.' He said he would play it once, with the words projected behind him. He covered the text on the projector, revealing a line at a time:

Have you heard the news?
   Have you heard the news,
   Some people win, but others lose
   Have you heard the news?

Have you heard about the woman
   Who's gone to outer space
   Have you heard about the runner
   Who's won every single race ...

Graham tried to cover his ears. He'd never liked guitar groups. Luciana was clapping along. Malcolm O'Reilly was smiling and nodding. Giles looked sideways at Luciana and started clapping too.

'Now it's your turn,' said Ryan. He proceeded to divide the audience into two halves left and right, no mean feat with two thousand people.

'Elizabeth told me he divided it into men and women in London,' said Luciana, 'But what with the audience here being ninety per cent female, he changed it.'

'So, this side sings the red text, the other side sings the blue text,' he announced.

Then he restarted the tape, singing loudly along himself, and exhorting the audience to join in, then the old pantomime routine of which side was better, and a reprise of the song with the whole audience. The voices lifted the rafters. He received a standing ovation, with Luciana being one of the first to leap up.

'Luciana,' hissed Francesca, 'This is the opposition! Sit down please!'

That was it. Ryan bowed, waved and left.

There was an announcement of a fifteen minute interval before Graham's talk, and there was a stampede for the toilets.

'Good Lord!' said Graham, 'There was virtually no linguistic content. The man's a complete fraud! What have songs got to do with teaching English?'

'Pronunciation, stress, rhythm, intonation, catenation,' started Luciana, 'Plus it reinforces the grammar in a memorable way, because then kids go home singing it, so ....'

'Try and say something positive, Graham,' said Francesca quickly.

'About what? Caterwauling?'

Giles intervened, 'You do mention the British and American difference over "Have you ever ..." and "Did you Ever ..." so perhaps you could slip in a gentle reference there.'

'Sing it again with "Did,"' suggested Luciana, only to be roundly shushed by Francesca.

'Are you writing my talk for me, Winthrop?' said Graham.

'Good gracious, no. Apologies,' said Giles hurriedly, 'But I sense that Babbit has sold a lot of books today.'

'It's a long walk to the bus,' complained Mavis.

'I'm not taking it back to the hotel,' said Gloria, 'Malkie's conference is just around the corner. I'm meeting him there.'

They were walking around the side of St. Peter's Square, or in Mavis's case limping lopsidedly. Her hip hadn't reacted well to the long wait in the queue to see the Sistine Chapel ceiling. Mavis nudged Gloria, 'Did you see that?'

'No, what?'

Mavis whispered, 'Those two priests! They're holding hands!'

The semi-circular cloisters were full of perambulating priests in the weak afternoon sunlight, mainly walking in pairs. Gloria peered in the direction indicated, 'I expect they're friends.'

Mavis shook her head, 'The sin of Sodom!'

'What? Holding hands?'

'It won't stop there,' affirmed Mavis.

'Italians are just more friendly. You see lots of people walking arm in arm. The young Arab lads often walk hand in hand at Malkie's school. There's nothing to it. They're young lads away from home.'

'They're priests!' said Mavis.

'The ones in the brown robes are monks,' said Gloria, 'I was at a Catholic school for a short time.'

Mavis looked worried, 'It's not natural. What do you think they do? I mean, when they ...'

'Use your imagination,' said Gloria, 'Come on, I'll walk to the bus with you.'

'It doesn't leave for thirty minutes,' said Mavis mournfully.

'Alright then, let's find somewhere for coffee,' said Gloria.

The bar was narrow, with just one metal table and two chairs. Luciana had said Italians were happy to stand for a quick blast of espresso. 'I'll get them, you sit down,' said Gloria, 'White or black?'

Mavis gratefully sank onto a chair, 'With milk.'

'*Buongiorno, due* … er … cappuccinos,' ventured Gloria. She looked up at the shelf behind the counter, 'No, um, *uno cappuccino* and … *uno vin rouge* … no, *uno* … *el vino tinto. Grande.*'

'*Il vino rosso,*' said the bartender.

'*Oui. Vino rosso. Si. Gracias mille.*'

The bartender shook his head and sighed, '*Prego.*'

Gloria took the drinks over and sat down, 'They always appreciate it if you try to speak their language. That's what Malkie says.'

'You're very brave. I couldn't,' Mavis took a sip, 'It's very bitter. They don't know how to make coffee here.'

Gloria took a deep swig of wine, 'The vino rosso's OK.'

'There are a lot of Italian-Americans on the cruise,' Mavis continued, 'Visiting the old country. They can't understand much more than me. They know all the please and thank you and good morning, and they know a lot of the words for food, but otherwise they're lost.'

'Where are your ancestors from?' said Gloria.

'Scotch Presbyterian and German Lutheran,' said Mavis, 'Chester was a Seventh Day Adventist. We both ended up as Baptists. I'd love to go to Scotland one day.'

'Don't call them Scotch, if you do. They get very arsy about it. Scots or Scottish. Scotch is whisky. I did Scotland a few times when I was dancing. We were alright, but some of the comedians had a hard time in Glasgow. Tough audiences. It's not true they wear nothing under the kilt either. Too cold in the winter. You see more kilts in London actually. No, it was great for us. Then I went into musicals. That's when I met Malkie, and then it was all acting not dancing. Mind, it was getting tiring what with my bunion playing up and the corns giving me gyp. You couldn't do it now, get into theatre just like that. It's all drama schools, but I had an Equity card from the musicals.'

Mavis sipped her coffee gain, 'I know! If I go to Scotland, I can call in and see you. Is Bournemouth near Scotland? You got to give me your address.'

———

Graham took his place at the lectern while the Gandolfini crone introduced him. He couldn't hear what she was saying, but the applause from two thousand people was disconcerting.

Graham coughed, 'Good afternoon, er, ladies and gentlemen. My name is Graham Donaldson. I am a humble everyday language teacher, like yourselves. I am not speaking to you from some privileged academic ivory tower. I hope I will not be a disappointment after such a dramatic presentation. I will not be singing songs, nor asking you to stand up and gyrate, and I will not be showing you colourful pictures. I am simply here to talk about grammar in the year 1977 in a serious way, just as you will have to next week in class, without the benefits of such luxurious equipment ...' he gestured to the speakers and tape recorder.

There was spontaneous applause.

'Good Lord,' said Giles to Francesca, 'A perfect start.'

Francesca nodded, 'I must say it is a surprise.'

'The bastard. He's not as bloody daft as he looks,' said Luciana, 'More than half of the audience are boring farts too so they'll like it.'

'I reluctantly admit you're right,' said Malcolm O'Reilly.

Luciana indicated Ryan Babbit, who was sitting at the front, 'Look at Babbit. He's sat himself right at the front to put Graham off. He must be fucking fuming.'

Malcolm laughed, 'It won't be a problem. Graham's a fellow who's never made eye contact in his life.'

———

There was a standing ovation at the end. Francesca got up from her seat and moved towards the aisle, 'Come on, we should be there to help Graham when Babbit goes up, as he certainly will'

Ryan had stood and was shaking hands graciously with the admiring Italian women either side of him.

The four of them got to the steps to the stage. Francesca hesitated, but Luciana was already ascending them at a fast trot. 'Come on, Graham,' said Luciana, 'Let's get you to a nice cup of tea.'

To Graham's horror, the ghastly girl was grasping his upper arm firmly and propelling him towards the wings. Good Lord! People would think he was associated with her in some way.

***

Malcolm found Gloria in the lobby outside the lecture rooms, perusing the gruesome oil paintings of martyrs.

'You can have enough art for one day,' she said, 'Whoever painted that must have been sick. Are they really doing that to him?'

Malcolm turned his head to one side to see it better, 'They are. What a vile imagination. You found the conference alright?' he said.

'The posters all over the outside helped. I had to walk Mavis to the bus. She was scared of walking on her own, maybe she thought she'd be accosted by a randy priest, or forcibly converted to Catholicism. Then she insisted on our address. Said she'd send us a Christmas card. God help us if she ever turns up.'

'It's highly unlikely.'

'Dunno. I don't think she's got any friends. The other Americans were keeping well out of her way.'

'Hmm. Just don't send her a Christmas card back. It will only encourage her.'

'That's too mean, Malkie.'

'Believe me, I'm right.'

***

Everything about the hotel was dingy brown from the 19th century brickwork to the chipped oak front doors, and the dour baroque décor in the lobby.

Francesca showed the sheaf of invitations to a young lad at the desk outside the restaurant, and they were waved in past the brown heavy curtains.

'It's the same every year. Gandolfini makes her students do all the waiting jobs and make the food. She tells them it will help with their English,' Francesca explained.

'It's a bit of a dump,' said Luciana.

'Shh ...'

'Champagne, madam? Sir?'

They each took a glass from the proffered tray.

'How long do we have to stay?' said Graham.

'We'd better do at least an hour,' said Francesca, 'I've booked a restaurant nearby for eight-thirty.'

'You must let me pay for dinner tonight,' said Malcolm, 'We've had so much of your generous hospitality.'

'Of course you may not. It is our pleasure,' said Francesca, making a mental note to remind Luciana to bill Patrick at marketing in England for Malcolm and Gloria, and the editorial department for Giles.

'It's more of that fizzy wine,' complained Graham, 'We've had it before. It upsets me.'

'Prosecco,' said Luciana.

Gloria drained her glass, 'Tastes like BabyCham,' she summoned the pimply youth holding the tray, 'Be a darling. Can you find me some vino rosso? There's a sweetheart.'

Giles took a sip, grimaced, and put his glass back on the tray, 'Me too.'

Malcolm coughed, 'Yes, a red wine would be most agreeable.'

'Lambrusco?' said the youth with the tray.

'No, just ordinary red wine,' said Luciana, 'Chianti or whatever. Lambrusco's a weak fizzy red. Gandolfini obviously doesn't want anyone getting pissed.'

'We have only Lambrusco.'

'Shit,' said Luciana, 'We'll have that then.'

'Ah, Graham!'

They turned. Ryan Babbit was approaching with a wide smile. He shook Graham's dead fish hand vigorously, 'Congratulations, Graham. Really, so well done. Good barbs thrown. I admired that.' He looked at Francesca, 'Come this way. We need a talk author to author, without publishers present.'

Graham looked from side to side, hoping for rescue. The fellow had put an arm around his shoulder.

Ryan Babbit led him to one side, 'Author to author. I hope you noted my nods and smiles during your talk. I gave you my full on appreciative attentive listening, not that I agreed with a word you said. We have to help each other.'

'I hadn't noticed you at all, in fact,' said Graham truthfully.

'Ooh. Bitchy! As was the remark on the privileged academics in ivory towers. Have you seen North-East London Polytechnic? It's a cheap 1960s pile of yellow brick and glass on the wrong tube line, populated by waiters and waitresses on day release. It's not fucking Magdalene College, Oxford.'

'It was not intended as a personal remark,' stuttered Graham.

'Fuck off. Of course it was. Good shot, but be very fucking careful if next time I'm speaking after you. Revenge will be sweet.'

'I'm sure that ...'

Babbit squeezed his shoulder, 'That's not why I wanted to speak to you. Two pieces of advice, Graham. First, never knock the opposition directly. It reflects badly on you and the opposition are fellow authors. I do mean me, and I do mean that. Secondly, I'm inviting you to join the Society of Authors. We need to stick together against those utter bastards,' his nod indicated the UUP party. Graham followed his glance. He breathed a sigh of relief. Giles was already heading towards them.

'Good evening, Dr Babbit. I enjoyed your talk so much.'

'Thank you. Please. Ryan.'

Giles smiled, 'Thank you, Ryan. Giles Winthrop. I am Graham's editor at UUP. I'm terribly curious. What do two leading authors talk about at these events?'

'Royalty rates,' said Ryan with a wolfish grin, 'And how to stop publishers screwing us.'

'Really?' said Giles in alarm.

'We were discussing how we were sweating our bollocks off so as to line the already bulging coffers of Eden & Churchill and UUP.'

'UUP is an educational charity,' protested Giles.

'Bollocks. Increased profit means better claret at high table in the colleges next year.'

'Actually, I have heard our UK marketing manager say that,' said Giles.

'Ah, yes. Patrick O'Toole. The homophobic Irish oaf. I have met him. Unfortunately.'

Giles demurred, 'Well, he is somewhat outspoken.'

Ryan smiled, 'Actually Graham and I were talking about osteopaths. With our heavy writing schedules, low backache is the bane of our lives.'

Graham was looking bewildered.

'Also how fucking awful this Prosecco is,' he glanced at Giles' glass, 'Is the Lambrusco as bad? Yes, I thought so. Have you noticed how that dried-up old battle axe Gandolfini is glaring at me? Let alone the poisonous looks from that arrogant ageing queen Ubaldini,' Ryan gave a little wave in their direction with a wide and patently false smile.

'We had something of a run-in with Ubaldini yesterday evening,' said Giles.

'Good. Well, fuck the lot of them. Dinosaurs. If you'll excuse me, I must circulate and receive the gratitude of my admirers. Do watch out for the eventual altercation. It should be fun.'

'We're leaving quite soon. We've booked a table,' said Giles.

'Well done. If only Elizabeth had been so wise.'

Graham watched him go, 'What a foul mouthed fellow!' he exclaimed.

Giles thought for a moment. Ryan Babbit was obviously more entertaining company than Graham Donaldson was. Nevertheless, Graham was his lot in life.

On their way out the student at the desk beckoned them over, 'Please … you will take your souvenir gift.'

The table was covered with small bottles of olive oil. Each had a yellow label with ROME CONFERENCE 1977 printed on it.

'It is from Lazio. Rome area. It is made from the Sabine Hills. It is certain the best olive oil in Italia.'

Francesca just managed to stop making a comparison with Tuscany, 'Thank you,' she said simply. She handed one to Graham, 'Now you will be able to make a comparison.'

Graham looked at it. What a strange country, handing out unsolicited olive oil willy-nilly to people with boasts as to its origin.

Malcolm took two bottles, and handed one to Gloria. 'I shall be able to compare too. Dear Gabriella gave me a bottle from Emilia-Romagna,' he turned to the student at the desk, 'Thank you so much. Congratulations on your English too. It must be very difficult with all these famous teachers. You're doing very well. What is your name?'

'Anselmo,' The boy flushed and smiled, 'Mille Grazie, Dottore. Please, there are too many bottles. Would you like another one?'

'How kind of you, Anselmo,' said Malcolm, picking up a third bottle.

Graham scowled. 'made from the Sabine Hills' indeed, and 'certain the best.' Did no one correct blatant errors anymore? Could O'Reilly not stop this patronizing friendliness to all and sundry? It was the last straw. He had made his decision.

'Hold on, Graham, I think my shoe lace is undone.'

Graham paused. Why should Giles imagine that he was needed to be present for shoe lace adjustment? The others were walking ahead towards the restaurant and the air was cold and damp.

'I just wanted a word in private,' said Giles.

'I see.'

'Have you given any further thought to our proposal? It might be an opportune time to tell Malcolm, and suggest that you take a sabbatical.'

'I'm supposed to give at least a full calendar month's notice. That takes us to January 1st.'

'UUP would compensate World English Centre for a full month's salary if you would agree to start on December 1st.'

Graham pondered, December was rarely a full timetable for any of the teachers. It was too short a month for the short courses, and only a few students started a three month course knowing of the two week break at Christmas. So it was mainly the remainder of three month courses. 'Leave it to me. Perhaps I should bite the bullet and sit next to O'Reilly.'

'Shouldn't I join you?' said Giles.

'Perhaps so.'

'Then I'll speak to Francesca about the seating plan. Excuse me ...'

Graham watched Giles trotting to catch up with Francesca. So he was left walking alone again.

Francesca pointed at the rectangular table with its six chairs, 'I suggest we change our seating this evening and break the man-woman seating rule. I'll take this end with Gloria and Luciana either side. Would you sit at the far end Graham? Then Giles and Malcolm can sit either side of you.'

'Good. Girl talk,' said Gloria, 'I'm gasping for a drink to take the taste of that Lambretta stuff away.'

'I'll never call it Lambrusco again,' said Luciana.

Graham took his seat, 'Now look, here, O'Reilly ...' he started.

Giles interrupted, 'Perhaps we should order our meals first and discuss this a little later.'

Malcolm O'Reilly was puzzled. Discuss what? He picked up the menu, 'What do you recommend?' he called to Francesca.

'I asked for an antipasto and wine on my way in,' she said. 'I've asked for *Fiori di Zucca e Carciofi Fritti*. These are courgette flowers and artichoke deep fried. Then for the pasta course, I'd suggest *gnocci alla Romana*, then for the main course the *Coda alla Vaccinara*. This is oxtail and quite heavy, and you may fancy a lighter dish.'

'Suits me,' said Gloria, 'Ah, the wine's here.'

The waiter cleared the pasta plates away, 'It will be about twenty minutes for the oxtail,' he said, 'Shall I bring more wine?'

'Please,' said Gloria.

'This may be an opportune moment,' whispered Giles to Graham. He was aware of Malcolm staring at them.

'Yes. Well. Look here O'Reilly ...'

Malcolm looked skyward, 'We really should be on first name terms after so many years.'

'Yes, yes. Malcolm then. Let us not beat around the bush. The thing is Winthrop and UUP here ...' he indicated Giles, 'Need me to start work on some Workbooks. Um. Immediately. They are apparently desperate for more *Intercourse* right away. Can't get enough of it. They suggest I take an unpaid sabbatical of one year, so you will be pleased to hear that I will be able to return to WEC after a year.'

'Immediately?' said Malcolm, 'No doubt you are aware that your contract stipulates one full calendar month's notice in writing? The Swiss office are sticklers on such legal matters. You are suggesting you leave your colleagues completely in the lurch, then you have the audacity to ask for a sabbatical?' Malcolm could feel the heat rising in his cheeks.

Giles leaned forward, 'We were suggesting December 1st. Obviously. Graham would continue at WEC until then.'

'Only if I want him too,' fumed Malcolm.

'UUP realise you might need an urgent replacement and we would compensate you for a month's salary.'

'And so while you've all been smiling and inviting us so generously to meals, in reality you were plotting this behind my back all along?' Malcolm realised the three women had stopped talking and were listening intently, 'Please give me a moment to digest this. I am unused to such treacherous behaviour. I'll deal with this, then I think Gloria and I should leave.'

Malcolm breathed deeply. He knew, and knew that Graham knew, how quiet December was. Most of the staff would only be on a fourteen to sixteen hour timetable. It was time they used to prepare for the next year though, particularly the incredibly busy January for students from Argentina, Brazil, Chile and Uruguay.

However, a return to a normal timetable load would cause mutterings from Barry Grant and the like. Then there were those applications from Euro-Lang teachers seeking the higher salaries at WEC. One leapt out: Natalie De Souza. Very recently returned from Brazil after an acrimonious divorce, and on a short temporary contract at Euro-Lang. She had mentioned they were laying her off for the whole of December too with only a vague promise of employment from Bernard Arnold for January. Natalie. She had a research MA degree in Portuguese with a thesis on Brazilian and mainland Portuguese differences. Three years teacher-training experience at the Cultura in Sao Paulo. She was highly personable. She had asked incisive, though somewhat aggressive, questions after Graham's talk in Bournemouth. Not only that, inevitably the Brazilians in January and February were sure to complain again that while WEC offered supplementary translation classes in French, German, Spanish and Italian, none were on offer in Portuguese, though in the winter months, Brazilian was WEC's largest nationality group. In fact, they could run Portuguese translation throughout the year if only they had someone to teach it. Yes, Natalie. Her letter was at the top of the pile in his desk drawer. He could telephone her on Monday evening. Not only that with Graham gone, he could offer her a permanent position and she would be a major addition to staffing the teacher training courses, starting with the January one.

'Right,' he said, 'Two months compensation from UUP in lieu of notice and to repay us for the inconvenience and re-timetabling. Graham will terminate employment on December 1st. My Swiss management will certainly not countenance a sabbatical, even an unpaid one, though of course if things do not work out you would be welcome to re-apply for a position. World English Centre is to be credited on the title page as the establishment where this material was written.'

'I shall be writing it at home, O'Reilly!' protested Graham.

'Based entirely on your research opportunities at WEC.'

Giles intervened, 'The credit is perfectly acceptable to us at UUP. We are willing to put that in writing.'

They both looked at Graham.

'I am owed two weeks holiday pay from the summer,' he said truculently, 'Plus having worked all year I will not receive my two weeks pay at Christmas.'

'Of course we will honour your already earned holiday pay,' said Malcolm, 'But we will certainly not pay for the Christmas break when we are closed. Don't push your luck, Graham. Remember if I were to give you one month's notice today, and that remains a strong possibility in my current mood, you would not be paid for Christmas.'

'This is most unfair ...' he started.

'It sounds fair to me,' sad Giles, 'Really, Graham. This tour has gone better than we expected. Orders are coming in. Go for it.'

'Very well. I accept the terms.'

'So you are now a full time author,' said Giles.

Malcom extended his hand. Graham stared at it.

'You shake hands at this point,' said Giles.

Malcolm shook hands and stood up, and put his napkin on the table, 'Now I think we should leave.'

Francesca hurried around, 'I am so sorry, Malcolm. We cannot leave it like this. UUP Italia knew nothing of this editorial business, I assure you. Stay. Eat. We have liked ... enjoyed so much your company. Leave as friends.'

'Treasured,' said Luciana, 'We've treasured your company.

Malcolm knew Francesca was lying, and he considered mentioning the obvious seating arrangement, but decided it was convenient to pretend to believe it. He sat, 'My apologies for my raised voice. I do hope I have not spoiled anyone's meal.'

'Of course not,' said Francesca.

'I enjoyed it, me,' said Luciana, 'You certainly know how to drive a bargain. You don't fuck about.'

'Isn't anyone going to pass me the vino rosso?' said Gloria, 'I'm gasping.' Luciana pushed the bottle across the table.

Malcolm sat and smiled as graciously as he could. Giles was obviously a slimy conniving bastard. It was a win-win situation. He was rid of Graham at last, and Natalie De Souza would be a major addition to the staff. Then WEC would get the title page credit, which was ongoing publicity and a link to UUP's academic reputation. He would enjoy recounting it to Schaffhauser tomorrow.

'You were magnificent, Malkie,' said Gloria, 'Really magnificent. Just like you were on *The Importance of Being Earnest* tour when those silly buggers playing Algernon and Ernest were taking in in turns to skip matinees, and letting the understudy do it.'

'Bridlington,' said Malcolm, taking off his tie and starting to remove his cufflinks. 'That's where it all came to a head on the Wednesday afternoon. You can't have a sore throat coming every Wednesday morning that's miraculously cured by the evening performance. And didn't he do well after I sacked Algernon? I like to think I jump-started his career. From assistant stage manager and understudy in Bridlington to the West End.'

'He was on *Coronation Street* last week. What are you going to do about tomorrow? With the car picking us up at the airport. Will we still have to take Graham back with us?'

'I suppose so. One must be civilised. I don't wish to appear petty in victory.'

'Well, tonight you were the Malkie I remember. Come here ... '

Graham looked at his hand. It was still trembling. He'd never made such a momentous decision in his entire life. Would Mrs Read let him use her front parlour as an office all day? Perhaps the gift of olive oil would put her in a good mood, though undoubtedly she would consider it only suitable for medical purposes. She had seemed somewhat hard of hearing of late. She had barely responded when he explained non-defining relative clauses over dinner. Then how much ear wax did anyone have? Two bottles of the stuff too. There was the large one from Florence and the small one from Rome. He's added the small bottle to the bag he had been forced to drag around the entire country. Giles had mentioned prospective trips to Greece and to Spain the next Easter. They were the sort of places that produced olive oil, though did they also press bottles onto visiting authors? If so, hopefully, Mrs Read would get used to it. He would need to take a large quantity of antacids with him if the food were as rich as tonight's heavy repast. The nervousness resulting from being bullied shamelessly by O'Reilly in front of everyone, coupled with gnocchi and oxtail, had left him terribly bloated. The cheese, wine and grappa had not helped. It had been such a relief to reach the privacy of his hotel room and finally break wind. He deeply resented the loss of his paid Christmas two week break, even if Winthrop had suggested he would need to work through most of it. Cheated out of his just dues. That was it. Not that he needed the money. It was the principle. He sat on the bed. Then O'Reilly had more or less threatened to sack him! O'Reilly might rabbit on about the Swiss management, but he was the one who made the decisions.

'Rabbit on?' another animal connection. Where had he put his notebook with the notes on mule and horse? Ah, there it was under the bag with the olive oil.

Luciana topped up Giles' glass then Francesca's with grappa. 'You did it,' said Francesca.

'Thank you. Yes,' said Giles, 'It all went very well. Malcolm responded better than I'd expected him to in the end. We got off very lightly. I had been authorized to offer three months.'

'The dinners helped,' said Francesca, 'But of course they were both good company, and he is Director of Studies at one of the largest

schools ... you will remember to bill Patrick O'Toole, won't you.,
Luciana?'

'Hang on,' said Luciana, 'So were we just buttering him up?'

'Buttering up ... this I don't know,' said Francesca.

'Perhaps being pleasant and generous to someone in order to have
them agree?' said Giles.

'Or lubricating an area with butter before painful penetration?'
said Luciana, 'I assume you've seen *Last Tango in Paris.*'

'I really do not believe that's the origin,' said Giles, 'People have
said it for years.'

'Is that what we were doing though? Buttering him up? No
wonder he took umbrage,' said Luciana.

Francesca looked worried, 'This is now two idioms I do not
know.'

'Got pissed off? Took offence?'

'He was quite convivial at the end,' said Giles.

'Pleased to be rid of Graham, I'll be bound.'

'Three idioms!' said Francesca.

'There you go,' snapped Luciana, 'And you thought your English
was so perfect, Cesca. Oops! Now you've taken umbrage.'

'Sometimes, Luciana, we need to do these things in publishing.
You will learn.'

'I don't think I want to.'

Malcolm and Gloria were in the lobby with their luggage when Giles came out of the lift.

'Good morning, Malcolm, Gloria. Terribly early start. Did you manage to get some sleep?'

Gloria giggled, 'Not a lot.'

'Are you off already? Aren't you on the same flight as Graham?'

'We are,' said Malcolm.

'I'm three hours later, unfortunately, though I will head out to the airport at the same time and wait. Mine was a last minute booking. We'll be leaving in half an hour. You're most welcome to share a taxi.'

'Thank you, no.'

'On UUP of course.'

'Gloria and I wish to have ample time for the duty free shop,' said Malcolm, 'I'm rather hoping they sell Passing Clouds cigarettes, then there's perfume, and I hope to get some grappa, though I already have a bottle.'

'Well, it's been most pleasant meeting you. I do hope the conference was useful.'

'It was indeed,' said Malcolm, 'I found Ryan Babbit's talk particularly interesting. We will be adopting his book, I'm sure. Yes, most useful. We need something more dynamic and modern at Intermediate level now we no longer need to use *Intercourse*. Eden and Churchill, isn't it?'

'I get the point, Malcolm.'

'Good. Well, no doubt we will meet again.'

'I hope so.'

Graham was most put out. Giles was too far away from his flight time to be allowed through passport control so yet again he was left to fend for himself. A duty free shop. Perhaps he should avail himself of a bottle of whisky. The grappa all week had been most pleasant, but at home a bottle of Bells or Teachers blended whisky would no doubt suffice for an occasional nightcap. He looked at the display. Glenfiddich, Glenmorangie. Twice the price. He tutted. Yes, the Bells was the lowest price. Then again without duty, should he push the boat out ... an expression to note ... and try one of those over-priced brands? The Glenfiddich was in a triangular dark green bottle. He remembered it from Milan. It looked pretentious. No, the Bells went into his basket.

Then there was the souvenir shop. Possibly an ornament of some kind might be to Mrs Read's taste. The models of the Pietà were crude plaster and one had to wonder who would wish to have a sculpture of a nearly naked emaciated dead body on the mantelpiece. Then he nearly jumped out of his skin. 'I nearly jumped out of my skin,' he thought, yes, another expression for his notebook. There was a garish plastic rectangular picture of Christ with a crown of thorns. It was some sort of trick. As you moved left or right, the eyes followed you and the blood dripped from the thorns. He touched the plastic. There were ridges, and the picture looked 3D. Yes. By moving to the side, the eyes appeared to move and the blood dripped. It was most disconcerting. Totally unsuitable for Mrs Read. He chuckled, hardly the sort of picture you would place facing a water closet! He needed something less Roman Catholic. Mrs Read regularly attended the Methodist church.

There were some plastic figurines of Roman soldiers in a box. No. A die-cast model of a Fiat 500? A tin Vespa scooter. A plastic Alitalia aircraft? This must be the children's section. There was a brass model of St. Peter's basilica. Too Catholic again. Ignore the T-shirts with ROMA emblazoned on them. Then there was a china Colosseum with ROMA in red, white and green on the base. It would have to do.

What was the word? A knick-knack. That was one to add. He should find a seat and make some vocabulary notes.

Graham opened his notebook. It had been a most profitable week. He glanced through. He'd added 'rabbit (verb)' below 'mule' *person inveigled to carry contraband through customs*. He had surreptitiously torn out the newspaper story. It was folded in the back of the notebook. MULES ARRESTED WITH HORSE indeed. How could they have been that stupid? How .... Graham furrowed his brow. Good Lord! The dark glass bottle of olive oil! He was taken instantly in his mind to that restaurant in Naples. Men in black. Mafia. No, Camorra, staring at them. He shivered. A mule! The Garibaldi woman! No doubt she was an innocent. However she had carefully transported that bottle from Florence to Naples and delivered it into a den of thieves! What had been in it? Drugs doubtless. Heroin, or horse! And here he was in an airport with the other bottle. He was sweating suddenly. Years in prison. An Italian prison too, without a word of the language. Life in prison? No doubt a hot and sweaty cell. Stabbed to death in prison by complete strangers because he did not speak their language or understand their arcane rules? He sniffed in self-pity. Or perhaps he would be kidnapped upon arrival in London! That was more likely, after the bottle had been transported through customs. They would have to silence him obviously. He would end up buried under concrete below a motorway bridge. No monument for people to visit and grieve his loss. He sniffed snottily again, it struck him that there wasn't anyone to grieve his loss! Then do you grieve a loss or mourn a loss? You grieve *for* someone, but you simply mourn someone. Or is it mourn *for*? It had to go in the notebook. He sniffed again. So much erudition would be lost forever.

'Look out, here comes Graham!' hissed Gloria. They were sitting at the departure gate reading quietly. 'He looks terrible. As white as a sheet. Did they all spend the night in the bar?'

Graham hurried straight to them, much to their surprise. He was shooting glances from side to side.

'O'Reilly! Um, Mrs O'Reilly! Thank goodness I've found you.'

Malcolm put down his book. This was unexpected. Hopefully, Graham was not going to withdraw his resignation.

'I need your advice!'

'Go on.'

'It's a long story. It all started in Florence, yes, when we were in Florence. We were in this restaurant ... it was in Florence, and I had praised the olive oil, a soup, yes, olive oil soup. Laden with garlic. So the next day the proprietor insisted on giving me a bottle, and of course Miss Garibaldi ...'

'Francesca,' said Malcolm.

'Yes, yes. Just listen. Garibaldi was given one too. A bottle of oil. But she had to deliver hers to this extremely seedy restaurant in the back streets of Naples. It was crawling with gangsters. Mafia. Armed to the teeth without doubt. We were dragged along with her. Led into mortal danger! The owner said it was just a coincidence that they were there, but don't you see? They were there waiting for the oil! They'd clearly met there to receive it.'

'Why would they be waiting for the oil?' said Malcolm.

'Because it was not oil!'

'You just said it was,' put in Gloria.

'Now I see! Miss Garibaldi was friends with the first restaurant fellow. I assumed she was quite innocent. I'm not so sure on reflection, but now they've involved me! Don't you understand! I'm a mule! A mule!'

'A donkey, more like,' said Gloria.

'No, the oil! It's not oil!' he leaned forwards and whispered, 'They told me it was oil, but it must be horse.'

'Mule ... horse ... donkey. I'm afraid you're losing me,' said Malcolm.

'Horse oil? You mean liniment?' suggested Gloria.

'It's the criminal name for ...' Graham looked both ways carefully and whispered, 'Heroin. It's a bottle full of it. Look, it's here!' he indicated the British Airways bag, 'They want me to take it to England.'

'They told you this?' asked Malcolm.

'No, of course not. I'm a MULE. A person deceived into carrying contraband!'

'Show me,' said Malcolm.

'Here? Shouldn't we go into the gentlemen's toilets ... somewhere unobserved?'

'Certainly not,' said Malcolm, 'Give me the bag.'

Malcolm took out the bottle.

'You see, O'Reilly. There's no label!'

Malcolm pointed to one of the array of plastic carrier bags next to his seat. 'There's no label on my bottle of grappa either. It was a gift from a Sicilian chap. It's very local. They bottle it themselves. Probably tax free.'

'No label? Sicilian? Sicilian! That's the Mafia! Don't you see O'Reilly! You're a mule too.'

'Nonsense,' said Malcolm. He held Graham's bottle up to the light and moved it side to side. 'It's definitely liquid. It moves slowly, and so it's viscose. It appears to be oil.'

'They dissolve the whatever it is that they dissolve in it.'

'I'm sure it's oil. I'm also sure that Francesca is beyond reproach. I would trust her absolutely.'

'But say she was fooled too! Or maybe they kidnapped a relative, and threatened to kill them or ...'

'Graham, this fantasy is running out of hand. I never knew you had such a feverish imagination. If only you'd put it in your book.'

Graham shoved the bottle back into the bag, 'I know! I'll leave it here on the seat.'

'I expect they'll just bring it after you and say you've left it,' said Gloria, 'It happened to me once with a bottle of duty-free gin in Malaga. Larios gin. I was a bit sozzled, frankly.'

'I'll put it under the seat.'

'Certainly not,' said Malcolm. 'Italy has terrorist problems. You must be aware of that. Don't you remember the Milan bombings? Then there was a train bomb, and a car bomb. Let alone that this is a flight to Britain where we also have terrorist problems with the IRA. You cannot just leave a bag in an airport. There are signs everywhere. It will be assumed to be a bomb. The flight will be delayed.'

'What am I going to do?'

'We'll have it,' said Gloria, 'Malkie likes olive oil. I'm not so fussed myself.'

'You'll carry it through?'

'Yes, because it's just olive oil, Graham. Pass me the bag,' sighed Malcolm.

'I don't want it given back to me in England!'

'Understood. We'll keep it. You might as well keep the small conference bottle though.'

The O'Reillys were seated several rows in front of Graham on the plane. They'd filled their overhead locker with carrier bags. Graham clutched his notebook tightly. He glanced across the aisle. There was a burly fellow in a shiny blue suit. Black hair. Brylcreemed. Small moustache. Pockmarked face. Was that a scar? The man realised Graham was staring at him. He smiled and nodded politely, '*Buongiorno.*'

Graham froze. Of course! They had followed him onto the plane. Tracking him. Still nothing was going to happen until they arrived, surely.

There was a young couple in the middle and window seat next to him. 'Good morning, sir,' said the young woman, 'Are you English?'

'Yes.'

'Do you know London well?'

'No.'

'We will stay there three days.'

'I see.'

'Oh. And do you know Brighton?'

'No.'

'We are going to Brighton for study English. At the Euro-Lang school. Do you know?'

'There is also a branch in Bournemouth.'

'Is it good school?'

'I don't know. Please excuse me. I have work I must do.' Graham opened his notebook. The couple should have been sitting next to O'Reilly. The man would have engaged them in inane conversation for the entire flight.

After the lukewarm coffee and the chicken pasty, Graham got up and scurried to the toilet at the rear. There were three people in front of him. The nervousness was playing havoc with his stomach. The enforced use of the facilities was not a pleasant experience on a plane. He banged his head badly getting up. The tap covered him with a sudden gush of water. Then he couldn't get the door open. Finally he managed to slide the bolt and the door folded open. He walked out straight into the fellow in the blue suit!

'*Buongiorno,*' said the man again, with a smile.

That proved it. They were following his every move.

O'Reilly was waiting at the luggage carousel when he got there.

'A pleasant flight, Graham? Gloria's just popped into the Ladies. We find it best to avoid the loo on the flight.'

'Mmm. Yes, yes.' Graham kept glancing around. The fellow in the blue suit was standing on the opposite side of the carousel to him. He was now wearing sunglasses. Sunglasses? In the gloom of the arrivals hall? The man nodded to Graham.

'Hello, Graham,' Gloria had arrived, 'That was a relief. I was bursting, but you can't use the one on the plane, can you?'

'Mr Connor's picking us up in the Granada. You're welcome to join us,' said Malcolm.

'Who's Connor?'

'Mr Connor? Reg Connor? The handyman? He's been working at WEC longer than any of us. You must know him. Anyway, he's bringing the company car to collect us. I'm sure we can fit you in.'

Graham looked up. The fellow was still staring at him. Well, he'd see that O'Reilly had the goods. Then he looked down. Blast! The bag with duty free whisky! He was holding it. Of course, the man would assume that was the oil.

'Graham, I asked you a question,' said Malcolm.

'What?'

'Would you like a lift down to Bournemouth? I'm sure we can take you right to your door.'

Graham considered. He had intended to take the Rail Link. A shuttle bus to Woking, then the train. That would leave him alone at the mercy of the man in the blue suit, and no doubt there would be accomplices. The alternative was being stuck in a wretched car with the O'Reillys for two and a half hours. Was there safety in numbers?

'Yes, yes. If we all get through customs.'

'Why shouldn't we?'

'I don't know.' The carousel jerked into life and bags appeared and the belt started rolling round. The man in the blue suit picked up one of the first bags. Expensive leather. Then he picked up something which had been next to his feet. A violin case! That was where the Mafia carried their tommy guns. Al Capone and the St. Valentine's Day Massacre! Graham felt as if his eyes were popping out. The man gave a small wave and walked away.

'Ah, there are our cases,' said Malcolm, 'It's always mildly alarming waiting for them to turn up.'

Graham's case was just behind them. He grabbed it.

The O'Reillys were walking in front of him. They were laden with carrier bags. They were certain to be stopped at customs. They wouldn't fool the customs officers with a green bottle. Then what? Arrest? Would he have to intervene and explain? No, that would implicate him.

O'Reilly was chattering away as usual, strolling blithely past the metal tables in the green channel. Surely he'd be stopped!

'Excuse me ...'

The voice was behind him. He turned around, a uniformed officer was beckoning him, 'This way, please.'

Graham walked over to the table. His knees were trembling. The O'Reilly's were already through the exit. Thank goodness they were carrying the bottle, not him. He remembered the tale of the orifice searches! Surely not.

'Have you anything to declare, sir?'

'What?

'Anything to declare.'

'Me? No, no.'

'Where are you travelling from today?'

'Italy. Uh, Rome. Yes. Rome.'

'What's in the bag?'

'Just duty-free. One bottle of whisky.'

'Cigarettes?'

'I don't smoke.'

'Perfume.'

'I'm a bachelor.' Why was the fellow smirking? Surely there would be no facetious comment.

'Right. Would you open your bag please?'

'Is this necessary?'

'I asked you to open your bag.'

Graham watched the officer rifling through the contents. He even opened the hotel bag of dirty clothes. He picked up a book, '*Intercourse? A Guide for Teachers?* So what's this sir?'

'I'm the author.'

'I see,' The man began leafing through the book, 'Oh. Less interesting than the title. It's an English teaching book then.'

'Yes.'

'You can close your bag.'

Graham started closing it. He looked round. People were strolling through without being stopped.

'May I ask you, er, Officer, why you stopped me of all people?'

'We don't answer that, sir.'

'I was simply curious.'

'Well, if you must know, you looked incredibly nervous at the baggage carousel. We observe people. You may go now.'

Graham hurried out. The O'Reillys were waiting by the exit with a surly looking man. He looked vaguely familiar.

'Hello, Mr Donaldson,' the man nodded at him, 'You may as well put your case on the trolley with all the others I'm pushing.'

O'Reilly was peering around. 'He's gone,' he said, 'He had a limousine driver waiting for him.'

'Who's gone?' said Graham.

'Nicolo Pavone.'

'What are you talking about?'

'The violinist. Nicolo Pavone. He was on our flight ... the chap with the blue suit. He waved to us. I saw his picture in the copy of yesterday's *Sunday Times* that we were given on the plane.'

'They'd run out of newspapers before they got to me,' complained Graham.

'That's why we chose seats further forward. Pavone's doing a series of concerts with the London Philharmonic. I'd love to see the Max Bruch Violin Concerto. He's recorded it twice apparently.'

'He kept looking at me and smiling,' said Graham.

'Famous people do that,' said Gloria, 'All the time. They're used to people recognizing them and staring at them. So they smile back.'

'I had no idea who he was.'

'He didn't know that,' said Gloria.

'He put on sunglasses as soon as we landed,' said Malcolm, 'That's another ploy. If people make eye contact, they start talking to you. Sunglasses avoid the issue. Of course, Gloria and I met quite a few well-known actors in our theatrical career.'

'Nearly all lovely people,' said Gloria, 'Not like comedians. They're all miserable sods. Hands all over the place too.'

Malcolm took a sip of Chianti. They'd had Reg Connor stop at the supermarket after they'd dropped Graham in Sebastopol Road which had caused more grumbling. Malcolm had opted for two bottles of the most expensive Chianti in the shop. After all, they'd barely touched UUP's generous per diem. They'd managed to get a fresh loaf of bread, tomatoes and some Parmesan cheese.'

He had phoned Schaffhauser immediately they got in. He had concurred with Malcolm's suggestion that UUP's compensation should be directed partly to award staff bonuses for the extra work during his and Graham's absence. That should take the wind out of Barry Grant's trades union sails and he could announce it to the staff first thing on Tuesday morning.

Malcolm looked at the three small bowls, and dipped some bread into the first one again, 'Yes, I'm sure. They're all good. However, the Tuscan oil is definitely the best of the lot. Graham carried it all round Italy, too. He really doesn't know what he's missing.

THE END

Dart Travis was born on the island of Jersey to a French-speaking mother and an English-speaking father, which he claims gave him an early interest in the intrinsic lack of genuine communication between cultures. His mother, Denise Leniece, was an accomplished painter, who was fond of the works of Alexandre Dumas, and Dart said she was only dissuaded from calling Dart's three older siblings Athos, Porthos and Aramis by a delegation from both sides of the family (I don't believe a word of it). Whatever, she insisted on christening her youngest son D'Artagnan. Her Jersey landscapes were too bizarre to sell well locally at the time, but are now collected.

Dart and I first met teaching in the 1970s, and I take credit for persuading Dart that while one apostrophe in a name was mildly irritating, two plus an interCap was ridiculous. After a few days of trying to explain his chosen spelling (D'Art') to classes, D'Art' became Dart, and has remained so ever since.

We kept vaguely in touch through the 70s, and I received an occasional rude postcard from the various places where Dart had ended up teaching: The British Council in Bulgaria; the Oxford and Cambridge Language Institute in Phuket and The Kool Skool (sic) in Amsterdam. I met him once, in 1983 when I was in Viareggio, Italy and he turned up with his stunning Italian wife and took me to dinner. He told me he had taught in England again the previous year for a few months, and had tried to look me up but had failed to locate me. I gave him my new address, but the postcards petered out in the mid-nineties, and I often wondered what had happened to him.

So I was surprised to receive a barrage of e-mails with the manuscripts of several novels enclosed. Dart had found my current address on the internet, and he wondered if my small ELT imprint, Three Vee, was interested in publishing any or all of them. Dart's then location in southern Venezuela made communication difficult,.

I know the eras, and I can confirm the accuracy of the setting of these picaresque novels. Dart has researched the music and events that form the background to the stories so as to give a feel of the era. He also told me that he had persuaded long exiled colleagues to read the manuscripts searching for like, you know, kind of, modernisms, in the dialogue. The novels feel genuinely of their time.

I read them avidly, and it was with major relief that I realized that at least no character bore any resemblance to me. I know Dart had played bass guitar as a teenager, and done lights on variety shows in his summer holidays for three years, then lived through the May demos at university in 1968 and was a roadie for a rock band in 1969. We were working together in 1972. Dart was always a weaver of tales and the ones here are somewhat different to those he told me nearer the time.

Italian Affairs is the most recent addition, the fifth published of the English As A Funny Language Series. Chronologically, it's the second story, set in 1977. Readers had been interested in Graham Donaldson who is a minor character in *Foreign Affairs,* then a major character in the three subsequent ones. *Italian Affairs* explains how he became a famous author. I note that Dart avoided setting any of it in Viareggio.

Peter Viney, Three Vee Limited

https://darttravis.wordpress.com

The Sixties Quartet comprises four novels:

No Secrets To Conceal: Early 1966

Music To Watch Girls By: Summer of 1967

The Women Came and Went: Spring of 1968

Pulling Into Nazareth: Autumn of 1969

Plus related short stories. The first set pre-dates No Secrets To Conceal.

I'll Tell Everything I Know: Short Stories 1964 - 1965.

The second volume fills in some time gaps in the novels.

Rolling Down The Road: Short Stories 1966-1969

The English As A Funny Language Series

Foreign Affairs (1972)

Italian Affairs (1977)

Home Affairs (1982)

Greek Affairs (1985)

Japanese Affairs (1986)

Three Vee also publishes:

The Play At The Arts Centre by Peter Viney

Toby Hamlet by Peter Viney

Lament of The Frontier Guard by Peter Viney

A Weekend Away / A Week by The Sea by Peter Viney & Karen Viney